Rabindranath Tago...
and writer, as well as a musician. He wrote over 2,000 songs, numerous short stories, novels, plays, essays, poetry and dance dramas. Among his songs are the national anthems of two countries—India and Bangladesh. Tagore was awarded the Nobel Prize for Literature in 1913.

the CRESCENT MOON

POEMS and STORIES

Rabindranath Tagore

▼▼▼▼

Introduction by RUSKIN BOND

talking
CUB

TALKING CUB
Published by Speaking Tiger Publishing Pvt. Ltd
4381/4 Ansari Road, Daryaganj,
New Delhi–110002, India

Introduction copyright © Ruskin Bond
Edition copyright © Speaking Tiger 2017

ISBN: 978-93-87164-34-5
eISBN: 978-93-87164-16-1

10 9 8 7 6 5 4 3 2 1

The moral right of the author has been asserted.

Typeset in Adobe Garamond Pro by Jojy Philip
Printed at Sanat Printers, Kundli

contents

Introduction   ix

POEMS

The Home   3

On the Seashore   4

The Source   6

Baby's Way   7

The Unheeded Pageant   9

Sleep-stealer   11

The Beginning   13

Baby's World   15

When and Why   16

Defamation   17

The Judge   19

Playthings   20

The Astronomer   21

Clouds and Waves   23

The Champa Flower   25

Fairyland   27

The Land of the Exile   29

The Rainy Day   32

Paper Boats   34

The Sailor   35

The Further Bank   37

The Flower-school   39

The Merchant   41

Sympathy   43

Vocation   44

Superior   46

The Little Big Man   48

Twelve O'Clock   50

Authorship   51

The Wicked Postman   53

The Hero   55

The End   58

The Recall   60

The First Jasmines   62

The Banyan Tree   64

Benediction   65

The Gift   67

My Song   68

The Child Angel   69

The Last Bargain   70

STORIES

The Kabuliwalla   75

The Kingdom of Cards   87

My Lord, the Baby   101

The Parrot's Training   114

The Home-coming   120

Master Mashai   130

introduction

The name Rabindranath Tagore usually conjures up an image of someone very serious. He is the revered poet and Nobel laureate. But those who have read him know that he also had a playful and humorous side. It was a tender, emotional side filled with laughter and wit. This came through best in some of his poetry for children. In his lifetime, Tagore wrote hundreds of poems and songs, many of which he set to music himself. He also wrote dance dramas and plays, apart from short stories, novels and essays. In this large body of work there are some poems and stories that he wrote for and about children, which have been brought together in this volume.

Each poem in *The Crescent Moon* evokes the tender love of a mother and her child. Sometimes the mother is the beautiful land all around, and sometimes she is very much a human mother, calling out to the crescent moon in the sky as she holds her child in her arms in the darkening night. Some poems are about the sweet sleep that plays on a baby's eyes at night, and in another the mother wonders who stole sleep from her baby's eyes. Was it the Sleep-stealer who lurks about near the pond in the evenings?

Tagore also wrote a number of stories with strong child characters. One of my favourites is Minnie, from the story 'The Kabuliwalla'. Minnie is a smart, precocious child, and her unlikely friendship with the burly Afghan from Kabul is beautifully described. Perhaps since he surrounded himself with children of all ages, Tagore was able to get to the mind of a child and put down in his stories exactly how a child thinks, talks and reacts to the world.

The Tagore family was a large one and there were always children playing about, studying—or trying not to study! Tagore himself has written elsewhere of his disdain for all kinds of formal schooling. He quite hated the schools he was sent to; the rote learning that the children had to do, and the exams they had to write. For him, studying meant letting the mind roam free to imagine in order to truly understand what is being taught. He believed so strongly in this that he started his own school in Shantiniketan. His wife, Mrinalini, gave him much of her jewellery to sell in order to raise money for the school. At Shantiniketan he created the kind of school that perhaps even I would have been happy to go to! Here, classes were held out in the open, under trees, no one was punished, and there was no learning by memory. Children worked and studied according to their interests. They played games, did art and learnt all that is essential, without feeling school to be a burden. All these thoughts are shown very effectively in the story 'The Parrot's Learning'. What happens if you keep pumping words and concepts into students? Read the story and see!

It is interesting that Tagore's writing for children was not just poetry and stories, but also books that were meant to be used as textbooks! He wrote a series of Bengali language textbooks called *Sahaj Path* (Easy Reading), that started with simple rhymes teaching the alphabets and went on to teach sentences, paragraphs and rhymes. The books were illustrated by the famous artist Nandalal Bose, and are still used to teach children Bengali. Here is a little sample:

অ আ

ছোটো খোকা বলে অ আ
শেখে নি সে কথা কওয়া।

My introduction to Tagore, however, was not as a child reading such textbooks, or by hearing his songs. It was through a volume of poetry I discovered in a forest rest house during one of my stepfather's shikar expeditions. I was always averse to guns and shooting and preferred to see the animals and admire them for their beauty. Of course, no one else understood this, and I would stay back in the rest house when my parents and their friends went out shooting. Most of these bungalows had libraries, or at least shelves of books, that no one bothered to dust, let alone remove books from to read. It was from one such dusty shelf that I rescued a volume of poetry written by Tagore, translated into English, and read it over a quiet afternoon, sitting happily all by myself in the empty house. I later read many of his works, whatever I could find in various translations, but my happiest memory of reading remains that day in the middle of the forest, with the calls of birds outside and the distant roar of the jeep carrying away all the grown-ups so I could read in peace.

I hope this book makes many such happy memories for you too, as you read the beautiful poems and stories in it.

Ruskin Bond
Landour, Mussoorie

poems

the home

I paced alone on the road across the field while the sunset was hiding its last gold like a miser.

The daylight sank deeper and deeper into the darkness, and the widowed land, whose harvest had been reaped, lay silent.

Suddenly a boy's shrill voice rose into the sky. He traversed the dark unseen, leaving the track of his song across the hush of the evening.

His village home lay there at the end of the waste land, beyond the sugarcane field, hidden among the shadows of the banana and the slender areca palm, the cocoa-nut and the dark green jackfruit trees.

I stopped for a moment in my lonely way under the starlight, and saw spread before me the darkened earth surrounding with her arms countless homes furnished with cradles and beds, mothers' hearts and evening lamps, and young lives glad with a gladness that knows nothing of its value for the world.

on the seashore

On the seashore of endless worlds children meet.
The infinite sky is motionless overhead and
the restless water is boisterous. On the seashore of
endless worlds the children meet with shouts and
dances.

They build their houses with sand, and they play
with empty shells. With withered leaves they weave
their boats and smilingly float them on the vast
deep. Children have their play on the seashore of
worlds.

They know not how to swim, they know not how
to cast nets. Pearl-fishers dive for pearls, merchants
sail in their ships, while children gather pebbles
and scatter them again. They seek not for hidden
treasures, they know not how to cast nets.

The sea surges up with laughter, and pale gleams the smile of the sea-beach. Death-dealing waves sing meaningless ballads to the children, even like a mother while rocking her baby's cradle. The sea plays with children, and pale gleams the smile of the sea-beach.

On the seashore of endless worlds children meet. Tempest roams in the pathless sky, ships are wrecked in the trackless water, death is abroad and children play. On the seashore of endless worlds is the great meeting of children.

the source

The sleep that flits on baby's eyes—does anybody know from where it comes? Yes, there is a rumour that it has its dwelling where, in the fairy village among shadows of the forest dimly lit with glow-worms, there hang two shy buds of enchantment. From there it comes to kiss baby's eyes.

The smile that flickers on baby's lips when he sleeps—does anybody know where it was born? Yes, there is a rumour that a young pale beam of a crescent moon touched the edge of a vanishing autumn cloud, and there the smile was first born in the dream of a dew-washed morning—the smile that flickers on baby's lips when he sleeps.

The sweet, soft freshness that blooms on baby's limbs—does anybody know where it was hidden so long? Yes, when the mother was a young girl it lay pervading her heart in tender and silent mystery of love—the sweet, soft freshness that has bloomed on baby's limbs.

baby's way

If baby only wanted to, he could fly up to heaven this moment.

It is not for nothing that he does not leave us.

He loves to rest his head on mother's bosom, and cannot ever bear to lose sight of her.

Baby knows all manner of wise words, though few on earth can understand their meaning.

It is not for nothing that he never wants to speak.

The one thing he wants is to learn mother's words from mother's lips. That is why he looks so innocent.

Baby had a heap of gold and pearls, yet he came like a beggar on to this earth.

It is not for nothing he came in such a disguise.

This dear little naked mendicant pretends to be utterly helpless, so that he may beg for mother's wealth of love.

Baby was so free from every tie in the land of the tiny crescent moon.

It was not for nothing he gave up his freedom.

He knows that there is room for endless joy in mother's little corner of a heart, and it is sweeter far than liberty to be caught and pressed in her dear arms.

Baby never knew how to cry. He dwelt in the land of perfect bliss.

It is not for nothing he has chosen to shed tears.

Though with the smile of his dear face he draws mother's yearning heart to him, yet his little cries over tiny troubles weave the double bond of pity and love.

the unheeded pageant

Ah, who was it coloured that little frock, my child,
and covered your sweet limbs with that little red
tunic?

You have come out in the morning to play in the
courtyard, tottering and tumbling as you run.

But who was it coloured that little frock, my
child?

What is it makes you laugh, my little life-bud?

Mother smiles at you standing on the threshold.

She claps her hands and her bracelets jingle, and
you dance with your bamboo stick in your hand like
a tiny little shepherd.

But what is it makes you laugh, my little life-bud?

O beggar, what do you beg for, clinging to your
mother's neck with both your hands?

O greedy heart, shall I pluck the world like a fruit from the sky to place it on your little rosy palm?

O beggar, what are you begging for?

The wind carries away in glee the tinkling of your anklet bells.

The sun smiles and watches your toilet. The sky watches over you when you sleep in your mother's arms, and the morning comes tiptoe to your bed and kisses your eyes.

The wind carries away in glee the tinkling of your anklet bells.

The fairy mistress of dreams is coming towards you, flying through the twilight sky.

The world-mother keeps her seat by you in your mother's heart.

He who plays his music to the stars is standing at your window with his flute.

And the fairy mistress of dreams is coming towards you, flying through the twilight sky.

sleep-stealer

Who stole sleep from baby's eyes? I must know.

Clasping her pitcher to her waist mother went to fetch water from the village near by.

It was noon. The children's playtime was over; the ducks in the pond were silent.

The shepherd boy lay asleep under the shadow of the banyan tree.

The crane stood grave and still in the swamp near the mango grove.

In the meanwhile the Sleep-stealer came and, snatching sleep from baby's eyes, flew away.

When mother came back she found baby travelling the room over on all fours.

Who stole sleep from our baby's eyes? I must know. I must find her and chain her up.

I must look into that dark cave, where, through boulders and scowling stones, trickles a tiny stream.

I must search in the drowsy shade of the bakula grove, where pigeons coo in their corner, and fairies' anklets tinkle in the stillness of starry nights.

In the evening I will peep into the whispering silence of the bamboo forest, where fireflies squander their light, and will ask every creature I meet, 'Can anybody tell me where the Sleep-stealer lives?'

Who stole sleep from baby's eyes? I must know.

Shouldn't I give her a good lesson if I could only catch her!

I would raid her nest and see where she hoards all her stolen sleep.

I would plunder it all, and carry it home.

I would bind her two wings securely, set her on the bank of the river, and then let her play at fishing with a reed among the rushes and water-lilies.

When the marketing is over in the evening, and the village children sit in their mothers' laps, then the night birds will mockingly din her ears with:

'Whose sleep will you steal now?'

the beginning

'Where have I come from, where did you pick me up?' the baby asked its mother.

She answered half crying, half laughing, and clasping the baby to her breast, 'You were hidden in my heart as its desire, my darling.

You were in the dolls of my childhood's games; and when with clay I made the image of my god every morning, I made and unmade you then.

You were enshrined with our household deity, in his worship I worshipped you.

In all my hopes and my loves, in my life, in the life of my mother you have lived.

In the lap of the deathless Spirit who rules our home you have been nursed for ages.

When in girlhood my heart was opening its petals, you hovered as a fragrance about it.

Your tender softness bloomed in my youthful limbs, like a glow in the sky before the sunrise.

Heaven's first darling, twin-born with the morning light, you have floated down the stream of the world's life, and at last you have stranded on my heart.

As I gaze on your face, mystery overwhelms me; you who belong to all have become mine.

For fear of losing you I hold you tight to my breast. What magic has snared the world's treasure in these slender arms of mine?'

baby's world

I wish I could take a quiet corner in the heart of my baby's very own world.

I know it has stars that talk to him, and a sky that stoops down to his face to amuse him with its silly clouds and rainbows.

Those who make believe to be dumb, and look as if they never could move, come creeping to his window with their stories and with trays crowded with bright toys.

I wish I could travel by the road that crosses baby's mind, and out beyond all bounds;

Where messengers run errands for no cause between the kingdoms of kings of no history;

Where Reason makes kites of her laws and flies them, and Truth sets Fact free from its fetters.

when and why

When I bring you coloured toys, my child, I understand why there is such a play of colours on clouds, on water, and why flowers are painted in tints—when I give coloured toys to you, my child.

When I sing to make you dance, I truly know why there is music in leaves, and why waves send their chorus of voices to the heart of the listening earth—when I sing to make you dance.

When I bring sweet things to your greedy hands, I know why there is honey in the cup of the flower, and why fruits are secretly filled with sweet juice— when I bring sweet things to your greedy hands.

When I kiss your face to make you smile, my darling, I surely understand what pleasure streams from the sky in morning light, and what delight the summer breeze brings to my body—when I kiss you to make you smile.

defamation

Why are those tears in your eyes, my child?

How horrid of them to be always scolding you for nothing?

You have stained your fingers and face with ink while writing—is that why they call you dirty?

O, fie! Would they dare to call the full moon dirty because it has smudged its face with ink?

For every little trifle they blame you, my child. They are ready to find fault for nothing.

You tore your clothes while playing—is that why they call you untidy?

O, fie! What would they call an autumn morning that smiles through its ragged clouds?

Take no heed of what they say to you, my child.

They make a long list of your misdeeds.

Everybody knows how you love sweet things—is
that why they call you greedy?
O, fie! What then would they call us who love you?

the judge

Say of him what you please, but I know my child's failings.

I do not love him because he is good, but because he is my little child.

How should you know how dear he can be when you try to weigh his merits against his faults?

When I must punish him he becomes all the more a part of my being.

When I cause his tears to come my heart weeps with him.

I alone have a right to blame and punish, for he only may chastise who loves.

playthings

Child, how happy you are sitting in the dust,
playing with a broken twig all the morning.

I smile at your play with that little bit of a
broken twig.

I am busy with my accounts, adding up figures
by the hour.

Perhaps you glance at me and think, 'What a
stupid game to spoil your morning with!'

Child, I have forgotten the art of being absorbed
in sticks and mud-pies.

I seek out costly playthings, and gather lumps of
gold and silver.

With whatever you find you create your glad
games, I spend both my time and my strength over
things I never can obtain.

In my frail canoe I struggle to cross the sea of
desire, and forget that I too am playing a game.

the astronomer

I only said, 'When in the evening the round full moon gets entangled among the branches of that Kadam tree, couldn't somebody catch it?'

But dada laughed at me and said, 'Baby, you are the silliest child I have ever known. The moon is ever so far from us, how could anybody catch it?'

I said, 'Dada how foolish you are! When mother looks out of her window and smiles down at us playing, would you call her far away?'

Still said, 'You are a stupid child! But, baby, where could you find a net big enough to catch the moon with?'

I said, 'Surely you could catch it with your hands.'

But dada laughed and said, 'You are the silliest child I have known. If it came nearer, you would see how big the moon is.'

I said, 'Dada, what nonsense they teach at your school! When mother bends her face down to kiss us does her face look very big?'

But still dada says, 'You are a stupid child.'

clouds and waves

Mother, the folk who live up in the clouds call out to me—

'We play from the time we wake till the day ends.

We play with the golden dawn, we play with the silver moon.'

I ask, 'But, how am I to get up to you?' They answer, 'Come to the edge of the earth, lift up your hands to the sky, and you will be taken up into the clouds.'

'My mother is waiting for me at home,' I say. 'How can I leave her and come?'

Then they smile and float away.

But I know a nicer game than that, mother.

I shall be the cloud and you the moon.

I shall cover you with both my hands, and our house-top will be the blue sky.

The folk who live in the waves call out to me—

'We sing from morning till night; on and on we travel and know not where we pass.'

I ask, 'But, how am I to join you?' They tell me, 'Come to the edge of the shore and stand with your eyes tight shut, and you will be carried out upon the waves.'

I say, 'My mother always wants me at home in the evening—how can I leave her and go?'

Then they smile, dance and pass by.

But I know a better game than that.

I will be the waves and you will be a strange shore.

I shall roll on and on and on, and break upon your lap with laughter.

And no one in the world will know where we both are.

the champa flower

Supposing I became a champa flower, just for fun,
and grew on a branch high up that tree, and shook
in the wind with laughter and danced upon the
newly budded leaves, would you know me, mother?

You would call, 'Baby, where are you?' and I
should laugh to myself and keep quite quiet.

I should slyly open my petals and watch you at
your work.

When after your bath, with wet hair spread on
your shoulders, you walked through the shadow
of the champa tree to the little court where you
say your prayers, you would notice the scent of the
flower, but not know that it came from me.

When after the midday meal you sat at the
window reading *Ramayana*, and the tree's shadow
fell over your hair and your lap, I should fling my
wee little shadow on to the page of your book, just
where you were reading.

But would you guess that it was the tiny shadow of your little child?

When in the evening you went to the cow-shed with the lighted lamp in your hand, I should suddenly drop on to the earth again and be your own baby once more, and beg you to tell me a story.

'Where have you been, you naughty child?'

'I won't tell you, mother.' That's what you and I would say then.

fairyland

If people came to know where my king's palace is, it would vanish into the air.

The walls are of white silver and the roof of shining gold.

The queen lives in a palace with seven courtyards, and she wears a jewel that cost all the wealth of seven kingdoms.

But let me tell you, mother, in a whisper, where my king's palace is.

It is at the corner of our terrace where the pot of the tulsi plant stands.

The princess lies sleeping on the far-away shore of the seven impassable seas.

There is none in the world who can find her but myself.

She has bracelets on her arms and pearl drops in her ears; her hair sweeps down upon the floor.

She will wake when I touch her with my magic wand, and jewels will fall from her lips when she smiles.

But let me whisper in your ear, mother; she is there in the corner of our terrace where the pot of the tulsi plant stands.

When it is time for you to go to the river for your bath, step up to that terrace on the roof.

I sit in the corner where the shadows of the walls meet together.

Only puss is allowed to come with me, for she knows where the barber in the story lives.

But let me whisper, mother, in your ear where the barber in the story lives.

It is at the corner of the terrace where the pot of the tulsi plant stands.

the land of the exile

Mother, the light has grown grey in the sky; I do
not know what the time is.

There is no fun in my play, so I have come to
you. It is Saturday, our holiday.

Leave off your work, mother; sit here by the
window and tell me where the desert of Tepantar in
the fairy tale is?

The shadow of the rains has covered the day from
end to end.

The fierce lightning is scratching the sky with its
nails.

When the clouds rumble and it thunders, I love
to be afraid in my heart and cling to you.

When the heavy rain patters for hours on the
bamboo leaves, and our windows shake and rattle
at the gusts of wind, I like to sit alone in the room,

mother, with you, and hear you talk about the desert of Tepantar in the fairy tale.

Where is it, mother, on the shore of what sea, at the foot of what hills, in the kingdom of what king?

There are no hedges there to mark the fields, no footpath across it by which the villagers reach their village in the evening, or the woman who gathers dry sticks in the forest can bring her load to the market. With patches of yellow grass in the sand and only one tree where the pair of wise old birds have their nest, lies the desert of Tepantar.

I can imagine how, on just such a cloudy day, the young son of the king is riding alone on a grey horse through the desert, in search of the princess who lies imprisoned in the giant's palace across that unknown water.

When the haze of the rain comes down in the distant sky, and lightning starts up like a sudden fit of pain, does he remember his unhappy mother, abandoned by the king, sweeping the cow-stall and wiping her eyes, while he rides through the desert of Tepantar in the fairy tale?

See, mother, it is almost dark before the day is over, and there are no travellers yonder on the village road.

The shepherd boy has gone home early from the pasture, and men have left their fields to sit on mats under the eaves of their huts, watching the scowling clouds.

Mother, I have left all my books on the shelf— do not ask me to do my lessons now.

When I grow up and am big like my father, I shall learn all that must be learnt.

But just for to-day, tell me, mother, where the desert of Tepantar in the fairy tale is?

the rainy day

Sullen clouds are gathering fast over the black fringe
of the forest.

O child, do not go out!

The palm trees in a row by the lake are smiting
their heads against the dismal sky; the crows with
their draggled wings are silent on the tamarind
branches, and the eastern bank of the river is
haunted by a deepening gloom.

Our cow is lowing loud, tied at the fence.

O child, wait here till I bring her into the stall.

Men have crowded into the flooded field to
catch the fishes as they escape from the overflowing
ponds; the rainwater is running in rills through the
narrow lanes like a laughing boy who has run away
from his mother to tease her.

Listen, someone is shouting for the boatman at the ford.

O child, the daylight is dim, and the crossing at the ferry is closed.

The sky seems to ride fast upon the madly-rushing rain; the water in the river is loud and impatient; women have hastened home early from the Ganges with their filled pitchers.

The evening lamps must be made ready.

O child, do not go out!

The road to the market is desolate, the lane to the river is slippery. The wind is roaring and struggling among the bamboo branches like a wild beast tangled in a net.

paper boats

Day by day I float my paper boats one by one down the running stream.

In big black letters I write my name on them and the name of the village where I live.

I hope that someone in some strange land will find them and know who I am.

I load my little boats with shiuli flowers from our garden, and hope that these blooms of the dawn will be carried safely to land in the night.

I launch my paper boats and look up into the sky and see the little clouds setting their white bulging sails.

I know not what playmate of mine in the sky sends them down the air to race with my boats!

When night comes I bury my face in my arms and dream that my paper boats float on and on under the midnight stars.

The fairies of sleep are sailing in them, and the lading is their baskets full of dreams.

the sailor

The boat of the boatman Madhu is moored at the wharf of Rajgunj.

It is uselessly laden with jute, and has been lying there idle for ever so long.

If he would only lend me his boat, I should man her with a hundred oars, and hoist sails, five or six or seven.

I should never steer her to stupid markets. I should sail the seven seas and the thirteen rivers of fairyland.

But, mother, you won't weep for me in a corner.

I am not going into the forest like Ramachandra to come back only after fourteen years.

I shall become the prince of the story, and fill my boat with whatever I like.

I shall take my friend Ashu with me. We shall

sail merrily across the seven seas and the thirteen rivers of fairyland.

We shall set sail in the early morning light.

When at noontide you are bathing at the pond, we shall be in the land of a strange king.

We shall pass the ford of Tirpurni, and leave behind us the desert of Tepantar.

When we come back it will be getting dark, and I shall tell you of all that we have seen.

I shall cross the seven seas and the thirteen rivers of fairyland.

the further bank

I long to go over there to the further bank of the
river,
    Where those boats are tied to the bamboo poles
in a line;
    Where men cross over in their boats in the
morning with ploughs on their shoulders to till
their far-away fields;
    Where the cowherds make their lowing cattle
swim across to the riverside pasture;
    Whence they all come back home in the evening,
leaving the jackals to howl in the island overgrown
with weeds,
    Mother, if you don't mind, I should like to
become the boatman of the ferry when I am grown
up.

They say there are strange pools hidden behind that
high bank,

Where flocks of wild ducks come when the rains are over, and thick reeds grow round the margins where waterbirds lay their eggs;

Where snipes with their dancing tails stamp their tiny footprints upon the clean soft mud;

Where in the evening the tall grasses crested with white flowers invite the moonbeam to float upon their waves.

Mother, if you don't mind, I should like to become the boatman of the ferryboat when I am grown up.

I shall cross and cross back from bank to bank, and all the boys and girls of the village will wonder at me while they are bathing.

When the sun climbs the mid sky and morning wears on to noon, I shall come running to you, saying, 'Mother, I am hungry!'

When the day is done and the shadows cower under the trees, I shall come back in the dusk.

I shall never go away from you into the town to work like father.

Mother, if you don't mind, I should like to become the boatman of the ferryboat when I am grown up.

the flower-school

When storm clouds rumble in the sky and June
showers come down,
   The moist east wind comes marching over the
heath to blow its bagpipes among the bamboos.
   Then crowds of flowers come out of a sudden,
from nobody knows where, and dance upon the
grass in wild glee.

Mother, I really think the flowers go to school
underground.
   They do their lessons with doors shut, and if
they want to come out to play before it is time, their
master makes them stand in a corner.

When the rains come they have their holidays.
   Branches clash together in the forest, and the
leaves rustle in the wild wind, the thunder-clouds

clap their giant hands and the flower children rush out in dresses of pink and yellow and white.

Do you know, mother, their home is in the sky, where the stars are.
    Haven't you seen how eager they are to get there? Don't you know why they are in such a hurry?
    Of course, I can guess to whom they raise their arms: they have their mother as I have my own.

the merchant

Imagine, mother, that you are to stay at home and I am to travel into strange lands.

Imagine that my boat is ready at the landing fully laden.

Now think well, mother, before you say what I shall bring for you when I come back.

Mother, do you want heaps and heaps of gold?

There, by the banks of golden streams, fields are full of golden harvest.

And in the shade of the forest path the golden champa flowers drop on the ground.

I will gather them all for you in many hundred baskets. Mother, do you want pearls big as the raindrops of autumn?

I shall cross to the pearl island shore.

There in the early morning light pearls tremble on the meadow flowers, pearls drop on the grass, and pearls are scattered on the sand in spray by the wild sea-waves.

My brother shall have a pair of horses with wings to fly among the clouds.

For father I shall bring a magic pen that, without his knowing, will write of itself.

For you, mother, I must have the casket and jewel that cost seven kings their kingdoms.

sympathy

If I were only a little puppy, not your baby, mother dear, would you say 'No' to me if I tried to eat from your dish?

Would you drive me off, saying to me, 'Get away, you naughty little puppy?'

Then go, mother, go! I will never come to you when you call me, and never let you feed me any more.

If I were only a little green parrot, and not your baby, mother dear, would you keep me chained lest I should fly away?

Would you shake your finger at me and say, 'What an ungrateful wretch of a bird! It is gnawing at its chain day and night?'

Then, go, mother, go! I will run away into the woods; I will never let you take me in your arms again.

vocation

When the gong sounds ten in the morning and I
walk to school by our lane,

Every day I meet the hawker crying, 'Bangles,
crystal bangles!'

There is nothing to hurry him on, there is no
road he must take, no place he must go to, no time
when he must come home.

I wish I were a hawker, spending my day in the
road, crying, 'Bangles, crystal bangles!'

When at four in the afternoon I come back from
the school,

I can see through the gate of that house the
gardener digging the ground.

He does what he likes with his spade, he soils his
clothes with dust, nobody takes him to task if he
gets baked in the sun or gets wet.

I wish I were a gardener digging away at the garden with nobody to stop me from digging.

Just as it gets dark in the evening and my mother sends me to bed,
I can see through my open window the watchman walking up and down.
The lane is dark and lonely, and the street-lamp stands like a giant with one red eye in its head.
The watchman swings his lantern and walks with his shadow at his side, and never once goes to bed in his life.
I wish I were a watchman walking the streets all night, chasing the shadows with my lantern.

superior

Mother, your baby is silly! She is so absurdly childish!

She does not know the difference between the lights in the streets and the stars.

When we play at eating with pebbles, she thinks they are real food, and tries to put them into her mouth.

When I open a book before her and ask her to learn her a, b, c, she tears the leaves with her hands and roars for joy at nothing; this is your baby's way of doing her lesson.

When I shake my head at her in anger and scold her and call her naughty, she laughs and thinks it great fun.

Everybody knows that father is away, but if in play I call aloud 'Father,' she looks about her in excitement and thinks that father is near.

When I hold my class with the donkeys that our washerman brings to carry away the clothes and I

warn her that I am the schoolmaster, she will scream
for no reason and call me dada.

Your baby wants to catch the moon. She is so
funny; she calls Ganesh Ganush.

Mother, your baby is silly, she is so absurdly
childish!

the little big man

I am small because I am a little child. I shall be big when I am as old as my father is.

My teacher will come and say, 'It is late, bring your slate and your books.'

I shall tell him, 'Do you not know I am as big as father? And I must not have lessons any more.'

My master will wonder and say, 'He can leave his books if he likes, for he is grown up.'

I shall dress myself and walk to the fair where the crowd is thick.

My uncle will come rushing up to me and say, 'You will get lost, my boy; let me carry you.'

I shall answer, 'Can't you see, uncle, I am as big as father. I must go to the fair alone.'

Uncle will say, 'Yes, he can go wherever he likes, for he is grown up.'

Mother will come from her bath when I am giving money to my nurse, for I shall know how to open the box with my key.

Mother will say, 'What are you about, naughty child?'

I shall tell her, 'Mother, don't you know, I am as big as father, and I must give silver to my nurse.'

Mother will say to herself, 'He can give money to whom he likes, for he is grown up.'

In the holiday time in October father will come home and, thinking that I am still a baby, will bring for me from the town little shoes and small silken frocks.

I shall say, 'Father, give them to my dada, for I am as big as you are.'

Father will think and say, 'He can buy his own clothes if he likes, for he is grown up.'

twelve o'clock

Mother, I do want to leave off my lessons now. I
have been at my book all the morning.

You say it is only twelve o'clock. Suppose it isn't
any later; can't you ever think it is afternoon when it
is only twelve o'clock?

I can easily imagine now that the sun has reached
the edge of that rice-field, and the old fisher-woman
is gathering herbs for her supper by the side of the
pond.

I can just shut my eyes and think that the
shadows are growing darker under the madar tree,
and the water in the pond looks shiny black.

If twelve o'clock can come in the night, why
can't the night come when it is twelve o'clock?

authorship

You say that father writes a lot of books, but what
he writes I don't understand.

He was reading to you all the evening, but could
you really make out what he meant?

What nice stories, mother, you can tell us! Why
can't father write like that, I wonder?

Did he never hear from his own mother stories
of giants and fairies and princesses?

Has he forgotten them all?

Often when he gets late for his bath you have to go
and call him a hundred times.

You wait and keep his dishes warm for him, but
he goes on writing and forgets.

Father always plays at making books.

If ever I go to play in father's room, you come and
call me, 'What a naughty child!'

If I make the slightest noise, you say, 'Don't you
see that father's at his work?'

What's the fun of always writing and writing?

When I take up father's pen or pencil and write
upon his book just as he does,—a, b, c, d, e, f, g, h,
i,—why do you get cross with me, then, mother?

You never say a word when father writes.

When my father wastes such heaps of paper,
mother, you don't seem to mind at all.

But if I take only one sheet to make a boat with,
you say, 'Child, how troublesome you are!'

What do you think of father's spoiling sheets and
sheets of paper with black marks all over on both
sides?

the wicked postman

Why do you sit there on the floor so quiet and silent, tell me, mother dear?

The rain is coming in through the open window, making you all wet, and you don't mind it.

Do you hear the gong striking four? It is time for my brother to come home from school.

What has happened to you that you look so strange?

Haven't you got a letter from father to-day?

I saw the postman bringing letters in his bag for almost everybody in the town.

Only, father's letters he keeps to read himself. I am sure the postman is a wicked man.

But don't be unhappy about that, mother dear.

To-morrow is market day in the next village. You ask your maid to buy some pens and papers.

I myself will write all father's letters; you will not find a single mistake.

I shall write from A right up to K.

But, mother, why do you smile?

You don't believe that I can write as nicely as father does!

But I shall rule my paper carefully, and write all the letters beautifully big.

When I finish my writing, do you think I shall be so foolish as father and drop it into the horrid postman's bag?

I shall bring it to you myself without waiting, and letter by letter help you to read my writing.

I know the postman does not like to give you the really nice letters.

the hero

Mother, let us imagine we are travelling, and passing through a strange and dangerous country.

You are riding in a palanquin and I am trotting by you on a red horse.

It is evening and the sun goes down. The waste of Joradighi lies wan and grey before us. The land is desolate and barren.

You are frightened and thinking—'I know not where we have come to.'

I say to you, 'Mother, do not be afraid.'

The meadow is prickly with spiky grass, and through it runs a narrow broken path.

There are no cattle to be seen in the wide field; they have gone to their village stalls.

It grows dark and dim on the land and sky, and we cannot tell where we are going.

Suddenly you call me and ask me in a whisper, 'What light is that near the bank?'

Just then there bursts out a fearful yell, and figures come running towards us.
You sit crouched in your palanquin and repeat the names of the gods in prayer.
The bearers, shaking in terror, hide themselves in the thorny bush.
I shout to you, 'Don't be afraid, mother. I am here.'

With long sticks in their hands and hair all wild about their heads, they come nearer and nearer.
I shout, 'Have a care! you villains! One step more and you are dead men.'
They give another terrible yell and rush forward.
You clutch my hand and say, 'Dear boy, for heaven's sake, keep away from them.'
I say, 'Mother, just you watch me.'

Then I spur my horse for a wild gallop, and my sword and buckler clash against each other.
The fight becomes so fearful, mother, that it would give you a cold shudder could you see it from your palanquin.

Many of them fly, and a great number are cut to pieces.

I know you are thinking, sitting all by yourself, that your boy must be dead by this time.

But I come to you all stained with blood, and say, 'Mother, the fight is over now.'

You come out and kiss me, pressing me to your heart, and you say to yourself,

'I don't know what I should do if I hadn't my boy to escort me.'

A thousand useless things happen day after day, and why couldn't such a thing come true by chance?

It would be like a story in a book.

My brother would say, 'Is it possible? I always thought he was so delicate!'

Our village people would all say in amazement, 'Was it not lucky that the boy was with his mother?'

the end

It is time for me to go, mother; I am going.

When in the paling darkness of the lonely dawn you stretch out your arms for your baby in the bed, I shall say, 'Baby is not there!'—mother, I am going.

I shall become a delicate draught of air and caress you; and I shall be ripples in the water when you bathe, and kiss you and kiss you again.

In the gusty night when the rain patters on the leaves you will hear my whisper in your bed, and my laughter will flash with the lightning through the open window into your room.

If you lie awake, thinking of your baby till late into the night, I shall sing to you from the stars, 'Sleep mother, sleep.'

On the straying moonbeams I shall steal over your bed, and lie upon your bosom while you sleep.

I shall become a dream, and through the little opening of your eyelids I shall slip into the depths of your sleep; and when you wake up and look round startled, like a twinkling firefly I shall flit out into the darkness.

When, on the great festival of puja, the neighbours' children come and play about the house, I shall melt into the music of the flute and throb in your heart all day.

Dear auntie will come with puja-presents and will ask, 'Where is our baby, sister?' Mother, you will tell her softly, 'He is in the pupils of my eyes, he is in my body and in my soul.'

the recall

The night was dark when she went away, and they slept.

The night is dark now, and I call for her, 'Come back, my darling; the world is asleep; and no one would know, if you came for a moment while stars are gazing at stars.'

She went away when the trees were in bud and the spring was young.

Now the flowers are in high bloom and I call, 'Come back, my darling. The children gather and scatter flowers in reckless sport. And if you come and take one little blossom no one will miss it.'

Those that used to play are playing still, so spendthrift is life.

I listen to their chatter and call, 'Come back, my darling, for mother's heart is full to the brim with love, and if you come to snatch only one little kiss from her no one will grudge it.'

the first jasmines

Ah, these jasmines, these white jasmines!

I seem to remember the first day when I filled my hands with these jasmines, these white jasmines.

I have loved the sunlight, the sky and the green earth;

I have heard the liquid murmur of the river through the darkness of midnight;

Autumn sunsets have come to me at the bend of a road in the lonely waste, like a bride raising her veil to accept her lover.

Yet my memory is still sweet with the first white jasmines that I held in my hand when I was a child.

Many a glad day has come in my life, and I have laughed with merrymakers on festival nights.

On grey mornings of rain I have crooned many an idle song.

I have worn round my neck the evening wreath of bakulas woven by the hand of love.

Yet my heart is sweet with the memory of the first fresh jasmines that filled my hands when I was a child.

the banyan tree

O you shaggy-headed banyan tree standing on the bank
of the pond, have you forgotten the little child, like the
birds that have nested in your branches and left you?

Do you not remember how he sat at the window
and wondered at the tangle of your roots that
plunged underground?

The women would come to fill their jars in the
pond, and your huge black shadow would wriggle
on the water like sleep struggling to wake up.

Sunlight danced on the ripples like restless tiny
shuttles weaving golden tapestry.

Two ducks swam by the weedy margin above their
shadows, and the child would sit still and think.

He longed to be the wind and blow through
your rustling branches, to be your shadow and
lengthen with the day on the water, to be a bird and
perch on your top-most twig, and to float like those
ducks among the weeds and shadows.

benediction

Bless this little heart, this white soul that has won
the kiss of heaven for our earth.

He loves the light of the sun, he loves the sight
of his mother's face.

He has not learned to despise the dust, and to
hanker after gold.

Clasp him to your heart and bless him.

He has come into this land of a hundred cross-
roads.

I know not how he chose you from the crowd,
came to your door, and grasped your hand to ask his
way.

He will follow you, laughing and talking, and
not a doubt in his heart.

Keep his trust, lead him straight and bless him.

Lay your hand on his head, and pray that though
the waves underneath grow threatening, yet the

breath from above may come and fill his sails and waft him to the haven of peace.

Forget him not in your hurry, let him come to your heart and bless him.

the gift

I want to give you something, my child, for we are drifting in the stream of the world.

Our lives will be carried apart, and our love forgotten.

But I am not so foolish as to hope that I could buy your heart with my gifts.

Young is your life, your path long, and you drink the love we bring you at one draught and turn and run away from us.

You have your play and your playmates. What harm is there if you have no time or thought for us.

We, indeed, have leisure enough in old age to count the days that are past, to cherish in our hearts what our hands have lost for ever.

The river runs swift with a song, breaking through all barriers. But the mountain stays and remembers, and follows her with his love.

my song

This song of mine will wind its music around you, my child, like the fond arms of love.

This song of mine will touch your forehead like a kiss of blessing.

When you are alone it will sit by your side and whisper in your ear, when you are in the crowd it will fence you about with aloofness.

My song will be like a pair of wings to your dreams, it will transport your heart to the verge of the unknown.

It will be like the faithful star overhead when dark night is over your road.

My song will sit in the pupils of your eyes, and will carry your sight into the heart of things.

And when my voice is silent in death, my song will speak in your living heart.

the child angel

They clamour and fight, they doubt and despair, they know no end to their wranglings.

Let your life come amongst them like a flame of light, my child, unflickering and pure, and delight them into silence.

They are cruel in their greed and their envy, their words are like hidden knives thirsting for blood.

Go and stand amidst their scowling hearts, my child, and let your gentle eyes fall upon them like the forgiving peace of the evening over the strife of the day.

Let them see your face, my child, and thus know the meaning of all things; let them love you and thus love each other.

Come and take your seat in the bosom of the limitless, my child. At sunrise open and raise your heart like a blossoming flower, and at sunset bend your head and in silence complete the worship of the day.

the last bargain

'Come and hire me,' I cried, while in the morning I was walking on the stone-paved road.

Sword in hand, the King came in his chariot.

He held my hand and said, 'I will hire you with my power.'

But his power counted for naught, and he went away in his chariot.

In the heat of the midday the houses stood with shut doors.

I wandered along the crooked lane.

An old man came out with his bag of gold.

He pondered and said, 'I will hire you with my money.'

He weighed his coins one by one, but I turned away.

It was evening. The garden hedge was all aflower.

The fair maid came out and said, 'I will hire you with a smile.'

Her smile paled and melted into tears, and she went back alone into the dark.

The sun glistened on the sand, and the sea waves broke waywardly.

A child sat playing with shells.

He raised his head and seemed to know me, and said, 'I hire you with nothing.'

From thenceforward that bargain struck in child's play made me a free man.

stories

the kabuliwalla

My five-year-old daughter Mini cannot live without
chattering. I really believe that in all her life she has
not wasted a minute in silence. Her mother is often vexed
at this, and would stop her prattle, but I would not. To see
Mini quiet is unnatural, and I cannot bear it long. And so
my own talk with her is always lively.

One morning, for instance, when I was in the midst of
the seventeenth chapter of my new novel, my little Mini
stole into the room, and putting her hand into mine, said:
'Father! Ramdayal the door-keeper calls a crow a krow! He
doesn't know anything, does he?'

Before I could explain to her the differences of language
in this world, she was embarked on the full tide of another
subject. 'What do you think, Father? Bhola says there is an
elephant in the clouds, blowing water out of his trunk, and
that is why it rains!'

And then, darting off anew, while I sat still making

ready some reply to this last saying, 'Father! what relation is Mother to you?'

'My dear little sister in the law!' I murmured involuntarily to myself, but with a grave face contrived to answer: 'Go and play with Bhola, Mini! I am busy!'

The window of my room overlooks the road. The child had seated herself at my feet near my table, and was playing softly, drumming on her knees. I was hard at work on my seventeenth chapter, where Protrap Singh, the hero, had just caught Kanchanlata, the heroine, in his arms, and was about to escape with her by the third-storey window of the castle, when all of a sudden Mini left her play, and ran to the window, crying, 'A Kabuliwalla! a Kabuliwalla!' Sure enough in the street below was a Kabuliwalla, passing slowly along. He wore the loose soiled clothing of his people, with a tall turban; there was a bag on his back, and he carried boxes of grapes in his hand.

I cannot tell what were my daughter's feelings at the sight of this man, but she began to call him loudly. 'Ah!' I thought, 'he will come in, and my seventeenth chapter will never be finished!' At which exact moment the Kabuliwalla turned, and looked up at the child. When she saw this, overcome by terror, she fled to her mother's protection, and disappeared. She had a blind belief that inside the bag, which the big man carried, there were perhaps two or three other children like herself. The pedlar meanwhile entered my doorway, and greeted me with a smiling face.

So precarious was the position of my hero and my heroine, that my first impulse was to stop and buy something, since the man had been called. I made some small purchases, and a conversation began about Abdurrahman, the Russians, the English, and the Frontier Policy.

As he was about to leave, he asked: 'And where is the little girl, sir?'

And I, thinking that Mini must get rid of her false fear, had her brought out.

She stood by my chair, and looked at the Kabuliwalla and his bag. He offered her nuts and raisins, but she would not be tempted, and only clung the closer to me, with all her doubts increased.

This was their first meeting.

One morning, however, not many days later, as I was leaving the house, I was startled to find Mini, seated on a bench near the door, laughing and talking, with the great Kabuliwalla at her feet. In all her life, it appeared, my small daughter had never found so patient a listener, save her father. And already the corner of her little sari was stuffed with almonds and raisins, the gift of her visitor, 'Why did you give her those?' I said, and taking out an eight-anna bit, I handed it to him. The man accepted the money without demur, and slipped it into his pocket.

Alas, on my return an hour later, I found the unfortunate coin had made twice its own worth of trouble! For the Kabuliwalla had given it to Mini, and her mother catching sight of the bright round object, had pounced on the child with: 'Where did you get that eight-anna bit?'

'The Kabuliwalla gave it to me,' said Mini cheerfully.

'The Kabuliwalla gave it to you!' cried her mother much shocked. 'Oh, Mini! how could you take it from him?'

I, entering at the moment, saved her from impending disaster, and proceeded to make my own inquiries.

It was not the first or second time, I found, that the two had met. The Kabuliwalla had overcome the child's first terror by a judicious bribery of nuts and almonds, and the two were now great friends.

They had many quaint jokes, which afforded them much amusement. Seated in front of him, looking down on his gigantic frame in all her tiny dignity, Mini would ripple her face with laughter, and begin: 'O Kabuliwalla, Kabuliwalla, what have you got in your bag?'

And he would reply, in the nasal accents of the mountaineer: 'An elephant!' Not much cause for merriment, perhaps; but how they both enjoyed the witticism! And for me, this child's talk with a grown-up man had always in it something strangely fascinating.

Then the Kabuliwalla, not to be behindhand, would take his turn: 'Well, little one, and when are you going to the father-in-law's house?'

Now most small Bengali maidens have heard long ago about the father-in-law's house; but we, being a little new-fangled, had kept these things from our child, and Mini at this question must have been a trifle bewildered. But she would not show it, and with ready tact replied: 'Are you going there?'

Amongst men of the Kabuliwalla's class, however, it is well known that the words father-in-law's house have a double meaning. It is a euphemism for jail, the place where we are well cared for, at no expense to ourselves. In this sense would the sturdy pedlar take my daughter's question. 'Ah,' he would say, shaking his fist at an invisible policeman, 'I will thrash my father-in-law!' Hearing this, and picturing the poor discomfited relative, Mini would go off into peals of laughter, in which her formidable friend would join.

These were autumn mornings, the very time of year when kings of old went forth to conquest; and I, never stirring from my little corner in Calcutta, would let my mind wander over the whole world. At the very name of another country, my heart would go out to it, and at the sight of a foreigner in the streets, I would fall to weaving a network of dreams—the mountains, the glens, and the forests of his distant home, with his cottage in its setting, and the free and independent life of far-away wilds. Perhaps the scenes of travel conjure themselves up before me, and pass and repass in my imagination all the more vividly, because I lead such a vegetable existence, that a call to travel would fall upon me like a thunderbolt. In the presence of this Kabuliwalla, I was immediately transported to the foot of arid mountain peaks, with narrow little defiles twisting in and out amongst their towering heights. I could see the string of camels bearing the merchandise, and the company of turbaned merchants, carrying some of their queer old firearms, and some of their spears, journeying downward towards the plains. I could see—but at some such point Mini's mother would intervene, imploring me to 'beware of that man.'

Mini's mother is unfortunately a very timid lady. Whenever she hears a noise in the street, or sees people coming towards the house, she always jumps to the conclusion that they are either thieves, or drunkards, or snakes, or tigers, or malaria, or cockroaches, or caterpillars, or an English sailor. Even after all these years of experience, she is not able to overcome her terror. So she was full of doubts about the Kabuliwalla, and used to beg me to keep a watchful eye on him.

I tried to laugh her fear gently away, but then she would turn round on me seriously, and ask me solemn questions.

Were children never kidnapped?

Was it, then, not true that there was slavery in Cabul?

Was it so very absurd that this big man should be able to carry off a tiny child?

I urged that, though not impossible, it was highly improbable. But this was not enough, and her dread persisted. As it was indefinite, however, it did not seem right to forbid the man the house, and the intimacy went on unchecked.

Once a year in the middle of January Rahmun, the Kabuliwalla, was in the habit of returning to his country, and as the time approached he would be very busy, going from house to house collecting his debts. This year, however, he could always find time to come and see Mini. It would have seemed to an outsider that there was some conspiracy between the two, for when he could not come in the morning, he would appear in the evening.

Even to me it was a little startling now and then, in the corner of a dark room, suddenly to surprise this tall, loose-garmented, much bebagged man; but when Mini would run in smiling, with her, 'O! Kabuliwalla! Kabuliwalla!' and the two friends, so far apart in age, would subside into their old laughter and their old jokes, I felt reassured.

One morning, a few days before he had made up his mind to go, I was correcting my proof sheets in my study. It was chilly weather. Through the window the rays of the sun touched my feet, and the slight warmth was very welcome. It was almost eight o'clock, and the early pedestrians were returning home, with their heads covered. All at once, I heard an uproar in the street, and, looking out, saw Rahmun being led away bound between two policemen, and behind them a crowd of curious boys. There were blood-stains on the clothes of the Kabuliwalla, and one of the policemen carried a knife. Hurrying out, I stopped them, and enquired what it all meant. Partly from one, partly from another, I gathered that a certain neighbour had owed the pedlar something for a Rampuri shawl, but had falsely denied having bought it, and that in the course of the quarrel, Rahmun had struck him. Now in the heat of his excitement, the prisoner began calling his enemy all sorts of names, when suddenly in a verandah of my house appeared my little Mini, with her usual exclamation: 'O Kabuliwalla! Kabuliwalla!' Rahmun's face lighted up as he turned to her. He had no bag under his arm today, so she could not discuss the elephant with him. She at once therefore proceeded to the next question: 'Are you going to the father-in-law's house?' Rahmun laughed and said: 'Just where I am going, little one!' Then seeing that the reply did not amuse the child, he held up his fettered hands. 'Ali,' he said, 'I would have thrashed that old father-in-law, but my hands are bound!'

On a charge of murderous assault, Rahmun was sentenced to some years' imprisonment.

Time passed away, and he was not remembered. The accustomed work in the accustomed place was ours, and the thought of the once-free mountaineer spending his years in prison seldom or never occurred to us. Even my light-hearted Mini, I am ashamed to say, forgot her old friend. New companions filled her life. As she grew older, she spent more of her time with girls. So much time indeed did she spend with them that she came no more, as she used to do, to her father's room. I was scarcely on speaking terms with her.

Years had passed away. It was once more autumn and we had made arrangements for our Mini's marriage. It was to take place during the Puja Holidays. With Durga returning to Kailas, the light of our home also was to depart to her husband's house, and leave her father's in the shadow.

The morning was bright. After the rains, there was a sense of ablution in the air, and the sun-rays looked like pure gold. So bright were they that they gave a beautiful radiance even to the sordid brick walls of our Calcutta lanes. Since early dawn to-day the wedding-pipes had been sounding, and at each beat my own heart throbbed. The wail of the tune, Bhairavi, seemed to intensify my pain at the approaching separation. My Mini was to be married to-night.

From early morning noise and bustle had pervaded the house. In the courtyard the canopy had to be slung on its bamboo poles; the chandeliers with their tinkling sound must be hung in each room and verandah. There was no end of hurry and excitement. I was sitting in my study, looking through the accounts, when some one entered, saluting respectfully, and stood before me. It was Rahmun the Kabuliwalla. At first I did not recognize him. He had no bag, nor the long hair, nor the same vigour that he used to have. But he smiled, and I knew him again.

'When did you come, Rahmun?' I asked him.

'Last evening,' he said, 'I was released from jail.'

The words struck harsh upon my ears. I had never before talked with one who had wounded his fellow, and my heart shrank within itself, when I realized this, for I felt that the day would have been better-omened had he not turned up.

'There are ceremonies going on,' I said, 'and I am busy. Could you perhaps come another day?'

At once he turned to go; but as he reached the door he hesitated, and said: 'May I not see the little one, sir, for a moment?' It was his belief that Mini was still the same. He had pictured her running to him as she used to, calling 'O Kabuliwalla! Kabuliwalla!' He had imagined too that they would laugh and talk together, just as of old. In fact, in memory of former days he had brought, carefully wrapped up in paper, a few almonds and raisins and grapes, obtained somehow from a countryman, for his own little fund was dispersed.

I said again: 'There is a ceremony in the house, and you will not be able to see any one to-day.'

The man's face fell. He looked wistfully at me for a moment, said 'Good morning,' and went out. I felt a little sorry, and would have called him back, but I found he was returning of his own accord. He came close up to me holding out his offerings and said: 'I brought these few things, sir, for the little one. Will you give them to her?'

I took them and was going to pay him, but he caught my hand and said: 'You are very kind, sir! Keep me in your recollection. Do not offer me money!—You have a little girl, I too have one like her in my own home. I think of her, and bring fruits to your child, not to make a profit for myself.'

Saying this, he put his hand inside his big loose robe, and brought out a small and dirty piece of paper. With great care he unfolded this, and smoothed it out with both hands on my table. It bore the impression of a little band. Not a photograph. Not a drawing. The impression of an ink-smeared hand laid flat on the paper. This touch of his own little daughter had been always on his heart, as he had come year after year to Calcutta, to sell his wares in the streets.

Tears came to my eyes. I forgot that he was a poor Cabuli fruit-seller, while I was—but no, what was I more than he? He also was a father. That impression of the hand of his little Parbati in her distant mountain home reminded me of my own little Mini.

I sent for Mini immediately from the inner apartment. Many difficulties were raised, but I would not listen. Clad in the red silk of her wedding-day, with the sandal paste on her forehead, and adorned as a young bride, Mini came, and stood bashfully before me.

The Kabuliwalla looked a little staggered at the apparition. He could not revive their old friendship. At last he smiled and said: 'Little one, are you going to your father-in-law's house?'

But Mini now understood the meaning of the word 'father-in-law,' and she could not reply to him as of old. She flushed up at the question, and stood before him with her bride-like face turned down.

I remembered the day when the Kabuliwalla and my Mini had first met, and I felt sad. When she had gone, Rahmun heaved a deep sigh, and sat down on the floor. The idea had suddenly come to him that his daughter too must have grown in this long time, and that he would have to make friends with her anew. Assuredly he would not find her, as he used to know her. And besides, what might not have happened to her in these eight years?

The marriage-pipes sounded, and the mild autumn sun streamed round us. But Rahmun sat in the little Calcutta lane, and saw before him the barren mountains of Afghanistan.

I took out a bank-note, and gave it to him, saying: 'Go back to your own daughter, Rahmun, in your own country, and may the happiness of your meeting bring good fortune to my child!'

Having made this present, I had to curtail some of the festivities. I could not have the electric lights I had intended, nor the military band, and the ladies of the house were despondent at it. But to me the wedding feast was all the brighter for the thought that in a distant land a long-lost father met again with his only child.

the kingdom of cards

I

Once upon a time there was a lonely island in a distant sea where lived the Kings and Queens, the Aces and the Knaves, in the Kingdom of Cards. The Tens and Nines, with the Twos and Threes, and all the other members, had long ago settled there also. But these were not twice-born people, like the famous Court Cards.

The Ace, the King, and the Knave were the three highest castes. The fourth caste was made up of a mixture of the lower cards. The Twos and Threes were lowest of all. These inferior cards were never allowed to sit in the same row with the great Court Cards.

Wonderful indeed were the regulations and rules of that island kingdom. The particular rank of each individual had been settled from time immemorial. Every one had his own appointed work, and never did anything else. An unseen hand appeared to be directing them wherever they went,— according to the Rules.

No one in the Kingdom of Cards had any occasion to think; no one had any need to come to any decision; no one was ever required to debate any new subject. The citizens all moved along in a listless groove without speech. When they fell, they made no noise. They lay down on their backs, and gazed upward at the sky with each prim feature firmly fixed for ever.

There was a remarkable stillness in the Kingdom of Cards. Satisfaction and contentment were complete in all their rounded wholeness. There was never any uproar or violence. There was never any excitement or enthusiasm.

The great ocean, crooning its lullaby with one unceasing melody, lapped the island to sleep with a thousand soft touches of its wave's white hands. The vast sky, like the outspread azure wings of the brooding mother-bird, nestled the island round with its downy plume. For on the distant horizon a deep blue line betokened another shore. But no sound of quarrel or strife could reach the Island of Cards, to break its calm repose.

II

In that far-off foreign land across the sea, there lived a young Prince whose mother was a sorrowing queen. This queen had fallen from favour, and was living with her only son on the seashore. The Prince passed his childhood alone and forlorn, sitting by his forlorn mother, weaving the net of his big desires. He longed to go in search of the Flying

Horse, the Jewel in the Cobra's hood, the Rose of Heaven, the Magic Roads, or to find where the Princess Beauty was sleeping in the Ogre's castle over the thirteen rivers and across the seven seas.

From the Son of the Merchant at school the young Prince learnt the stories of foreign kingdoms. From the Son of the Kotwal he learnt the adventures of the Two Genii of the Lamp. And when the rain came beating down, and the clouds covered the sky, he would sit on the threshold facing the sea, and say to his sorrowing mother: 'Tell me, mother, a story of some very far-off land.'

And his mother would tell him an endless tale she had heard in her childhood of a wonderful country beyond the sea where dwelt the Princess Beauty. And the heart of the young Prince would become sick with longing, as he sat on the threshold, looking out on the ocean, listening to his mother's wonderful story, while the rain outside came beating down and the grey clouds covered the sky.

One day the Son of the Merchant came to the Prince, and said boldly: 'Comrade, my studies are over. I am now setting out on my travels to seek my fortunes on the sea. I have come to bid you good-bye.'

The Prince said, 'I will go with you.'

And the Son of Kotwal said also: 'Comrades, trusty and true, you will not leave me behind. I also will be your companion.'

Then the young Prince said to his sorrowing mother, 'Mother, I am now setting out on my travels to seek my fortune. When I come back once more, I shall surely have found some way to remove all your sorrow.'

So the Three Companions set out on their travels together. In the harbour were anchored the twelve ships of the merchant, and the Three Companions got on board. The south wind was blowing, and the twelve ships sailed away, as fast as the desires which rose in the Prince's breast.

At the Conch Shell Island they filled one ship with conchs. At the Sandal Wood Island they filled a second ship with sandal-wood, and at the Coral Island they filled a third ship with coral.

Four years passed away, and they filled four more ships, one with ivory, one with musk, one with cloves, and one with nutmegs.

But when these ships were all loaded a terrible tempest arose. The ships were all of them sunk, with their cloves and nutmeg, and musk and ivory, and coral and sandal-wood and conchs. But the ship with the Three Companions struck on an island reef, buried them safe ashore, and itself broke in pieces.

This was the famous Island of Cards, where lived the Ace and King and Queen and Knave, with the Nines and Tens and all the other members—according to the Rules.

III

Up till now there had been nothing to disturb that island's stillness. No new thing had ever happened. No discussion had ever been held.

And then, of a sudden, the Three Companions appeared, thrown up by the sea,—and the Great Debate began. There were three main points of dispute.

First, to what caste should these unclassed strangers belong? Should they rank with the Court Cards? Or were they merely lower-caste people, to be ranked with the Nines and Tens? No precedent could be quoted to decide this weighty question.

Secondly, what was their clan? Had they the fairer hue and bright complexion of the Hearts, or was theirs the darker complexion of the Clubs? Over this question there were interminable disputes. The whole marriage system of the island, with its intricate regulations, would depend on its nice adjustment.

Thirdly, what food should they take? With whom should they live and sleep? And should their heads be placed south-west, north-west, or only north-east? In all the Kingdom of Cards a series of problems so vital and critical had never been debated before.

But the Three Companions grew desperately hungry. They had to get food in some way or other. So while this debate went on, with its interminable silence and pauses, and while the Aces called their own meeting, and formed themselves into a Committee, to find some obsolete dealing with the question, the Three Companions themselves were eating all they could find, and drinking out of every vessel, and breaking all regulations.

Even the Twos and Threes were shocked at this outrageous behaviour. The Threes said, 'Brother Twos, these people are openly shameless!' And the Twos said: 'Brother Threes, they are evidently of lower caste than ourselves!' After their meal was over, the Three Companions went for a stroll in the city.

When they saw the ponderous people moving in their dismal processions with prim and solemn faces, then the Prince turned to the Son of the Merchant and the Son of the Kotwal, and threw back his head, and gave one stupendous laugh.

Down Royal Street and across Ace Square and along the Knave Embankment ran the quiver of this strange, unheard-of laughter, the laughter that, amazed at itself, expired in the vast vacuum of silence.

The Son of the Kotwal and the Son of the Merchant were chilled through to the bone by the ghost-like stillness around them. They turned to the Prince, and said: 'Comrade, let us away. Let us not stop for a moment in this awful land of ghosts.'

But the Prince said: 'Comrades, these people resemble men, so I am going to find out, by shaking them upside down and outside in, whether they have a single drop of warm living blood left in their veins.'

IV

The days passed one by one, and the placid existence of the Island went on almost without a ripple. The Three Companions obeyed no rules nor regulations. They never did anything correctly either in sitting or standing or turning themselves round or lying on their back. On the contrary, wherever they saw these things going on precisely and exactly according to the Rules, they gave way to inordinate laughter. They remained unimpressed altogether by the eternal gravity of those eternal regulations.

One day the great Court Cards came to the Son of the Kotwal and the Son of the Merchant and the Prince.

'Why,' they asked slowly, 'are you not moving according to the Rules?'

The Three Companions answered: 'Because that is our Ichcha (wish).'

The great Court Cards with hollow, cavernous voices, as if slowly awakening from an age-long dream, said together: 'Ich-cha! And pray who is Ich-cha?'

They could not understand who Ichcha was then, but the whole island was to understand it by-and-by. The first glimmer of light passed the threshold of their minds when they found out, through watching the actions of the Prince, that they might move in a straight line in an opposite direction from the one in which they had always gone before. Then they made another startling discovery, that there was another side to the Cards which they had never yet noticed with attention. This was the beginning of the change.

Now that the change had begun, the Three Companions were able to initiate them more and more deeply into the mysteries of Ichcha. The Cards gradually became aware that life was not bound by regulations. They began to feel a secret satisfaction in the kingly power of choosing for themselves.

But with this first impact of Ichcha the whole pack of cards began to totter slowly, and then tumble down to the ground. The scene was like that of some huge python awaking from a long sleep, as it slowly unfolds its numberless coils with a quiver that runs through its whole frame.

V

Hitherto the Queens of Spades and Clubs and Diamonds and Hearts had remained behind curtains with eyes that gazed vacantly into space, or else remained fixed upon the ground.

And now, all of a sudden, on an afternoon in spring the Queen of Hearts from the balcony raised her dark eyebrows for a moment, and cast a single glance upon the Prince from the corner of her eye.

'Great God,' cried the Prince, 'I thought they were all painted images. But I am wrong. They are women after all.'

Then the young Prince called to his side his two Companions, and said in a meditative voice, 'My comrades! There is a charm about these ladies that I never noticed before. When I saw that glance of the Queen's dark, luminous eyes, brightening with new emotion, it seemed to me like the first faint streak of dawn in a newly created world.'

The two Companions smiled a knowing smile, and said: 'Is that really so, Prince?'

And the poor Queen of Hearts from that day went from bad to worse. She began to forget all rules in a truly scandalous manner. If, for instance, her place in the row was beside the Knave, she suddenly found herself quite accidentally standing beside the Prince instead. At this, the Knave, with motionless face and solemn voice, would say: 'Queen, you have made a mistake.'

And the poor Queen of Hearts' red cheeks would get redder than ever. But the Prince would come gallantly to her rescue and say: 'No! There is no mistake. From to-day I am going to be Knave!'

Now it came to pass that, while every one was trying to correct the improprieties of the guilty Queen of Hearts, they began to make mistakes themselves. The Aces found themselves elbowed out by the Kings. The Kings got muddled up with the Knaves. The Nines and Tens assumed airs as though they belonged to the Great Court Cards. The Twos and Threes were found secretly taking the places specially reserved for the Fours and Fives. Confusion had never been so confounded before.

Many spring seasons had come and gone in that Island of Cards. The Kokil, the bird of Spring, had sung its song year after year. But it had never stirred the blood as it stirred it now. In days gone by the sea had sung its tireless melody. But, then, it had proclaimed only the inflexible monotony of the Rule. And suddenly its waves were telling, through all their flashing light and luminous shade and myriad voices, the deepest yearnings of the heart of love!

VI

Where are vanished now their prim, round, regular, complacent features? Here is a face full of love-sick longing. Here is a heart beating wild with regrets. Here is a mind racked sore with doubts. Music and sighing, and smiles and tears, are filling the air. Life is throbbing; hearts are breaking; passions are kindling.

Every one is now thinking of his own appearance, and comparing himself with others. The Ace of Clubs is musing to himself, that the King of Spades may be just passably good-looking. 'But,' says he, 'when I walk down the street you have only to see how people's eyes turn towards me.' The King of Spades is saying; 'Why on earth is that Ace of Clubs always straining his neck and strutting about like a peacock? He imagines all the Queens are dying of love for him, while the real fact is—' Here he pauses, and examines his face in the glass.

But the Queens were the worst of all. They began to spend all their time in dressing themselves up to the Nines. And the Nines would become their hopeless and abject slaves. But their cutting remarks about one another were more shocking still.

So the young men would sit listless on the leaves under the trees, lolling with outstretched limbs in the forest shade. And the young maidens, dressed in pale-blue robes, would come walking accidentally to the same shade of the same forest by the same trees, and turn their eyes as though they saw no one there, and look as though they came out to see nothing at all. And then one young man more forward than the rest, in a fit of madness, would dare to go near to a maiden in blue. But, as he drew near, speech would forsake him. He would stand there tongue-tied and foolish, and the favourable moment would pass.

The Kokil birds were singing in the boughs overhead. The mischievous South wind was blowing; it disarrayed the hair, it whispered in the ear, and stirred the music in the blood. The leaves of the trees were murmuring with rustling delight. And the ceaseless sound of the ocean made all the mute longings of the heart of man and maid surge backwards and forwards on the full springtide of love.

The Three Companions had brought into the dried-up channels of the Kingdom of Cards the full flood-tide of a new life.

VII

And, though the tide was full, there was a pause as though the rising waters would not break into foam but remain suspended for ever. There were no outspoken words, only a cautious going forward one step and receding two. All seemed busy heaping up their unfulfilled desires like castles in the air, or fortresses of sand. They were pale and speechless, their eyes were burning, their lips trembling with unspoken secrets.

The Prince saw what was wrong. He summoned every one on the Island and said: 'Bring hither the flutes and the cymbals, the pipes and drums. Let all be played together, and raise loud shouts of rejoicing. For the Queen of Hearts this very night is going to choose her Mate!'

So the Tens and Nines began to blow on their flutes and pipes; the Eights and Sevens played on their sackbuts and viols; and even the Twos and Threes began to beat madly on their drums.

When this tumultous gust of music came, it swept away at one blast all those sighings and mopings. And then what a torrent of laughter and words poured forth! There were daring proposals and locking refusals, and gossip and chatter, and jests and merriment. It was like the swaying and shaking, and rustling and soughing, in a summer gale, of a million leaves and branches in the depth of the primeval forest.

But the Queen of Hearts, in a rose-red robe, sat silent in the shadow of her secret bower, and listened to the great uproarious sound of music and mirth, that came floating towards her. She shut her eyes, and dreamt her dream of lore. And when she opened them she found the Prince seated on the ground before her gazing up at her face. And she covered her eyes with both hands, and shrank back quivering with an inward tumult of joy.

And the Prince passed the whole day alone, walking by the side of the surging sea. He carried in his mind that startled look, that shrinking gesture of the Queen, and his heart beat high with hope.

That night the serried, gaily-dressed ranks of young men and maidens waited with smiling faces at the Palace Gates. The Palace Hall was lighted with fairy lamps and festooned with the flowers of spring. Slowly the Queen of Hearts entered, and the whole assembly rose to greet her. With a jasmine garland in her hand, she stood before the Prince with downcast eyes. In her lowly bashfulness she could hardly raise the garland to the neck of the Mate she had chosen. But the Prince bowed his head, and the garland slipped to its place. The assembly of youths and maidens had waited her choice with eager, expectant hush. And when the choice was made, the whole vast concourse rocked and swayed with a tumult of wild delight. And the sound of their shouts was heard in every part of the island, and by ships far out at sea. Never had such a shout been raised in the Kingdom of Cards before.

And they carried the Prince and his Bride, and seated them on the throne, and crowned them then and there in the Ancient Island of Cards.

And the sorrowing Mother Queen, on the far-off island shore on the other side of the sea, came sailing to her son's new kingdom in a ship adorned with gold.

And the citizens are no longer regulated according to the Rules, but are good or bad, or both, according to their Ichcha.

my lord, the baby

Raicharan was twelve years old when he came as a servant to his master's house. He belonged to the same caste as his master, and was given his master's little son to nurse. As time went on the boy left Raicharan's arms to go to school. From school he went on to college, and after college he entered the judicial service. Always, until he married, Raicharan was his sole attendant.

But, when a mistress came into the house, Raicharan found two masters instead of one. All his former influence passed to the new mistress. This was compensated for by a fresh arrival. Anukul had a son born to him, and Raicharan by his unsparing attentions soon got a complete hold over the child. He used to toss him up in his arms, call to him in absurd baby language, put his face close to the baby's and draw it away again with a grin.

Presently the child was able to crawl and cross the doorway. When Raicharan went to catch him, he would scream with mischievous laughter and make for safety. Raicharan was amazed at the profound skill and exact judgement the baby showed when pursued. He would say to his mistress with a look of awe and mystery: 'Your son will be a judge some day.'

New wonders came in their turn. When the baby began to toddle, that was to Raicharan an epoch in human history. When he called his father Ba-ba and his mother Ma-ma and Raicharan Chan-na, then Raicharan's ecstasy knew no bounds. He went out to tell the news to all the world.

After a while Raicharan was asked to show his ingenuity in other ways. He had, for instance, to play the part of a horse, holding the reins between his teeth and prancing with his feet. He had also to wrestle with his little charge, and if he could not, by a wrestler's trick, fall on his back defeated at the end, a great outcry was certain.

About this time Anukul was transferred to a district on the banks of the Padma. On his way through Calcutta he bought his son a little go-cart. He bought him also a yellow satin waistcoat, a gold-laced cap, and some gold bracelets and anklets. Raicharan was wont to take these out, and put them on his little charge with ceremonial pride, whenever they went for a walk.

Then came the rainy season, and day after day the rain poured down in torrents. The hungry river, like an enormous serpent, swallowed down terraces, villages, cornfields, and covered with its flood the tall grasses and wild casuarinas on the sand-banks. From time to time there was a deep thud, as the river-banks crumbled. The unceasing roar of the rain current could be heard from far away. Masses of foam, carried swiftly past, proved to the eye the swiftness of the stream.

One afternoon the rain cleared. It was cloudy, but cool and bright. Raicharan's little despot did not want to stay in on such a fine afternoon. His lordship climbed into the go-cart. Raicharan, between the shafts, dragged him slowly along till he reached the rice-fields on the banks of the river. There was no one in the fields, and no boat on the stream. Across the water, on the farther side, the clouds were rifted in the west. The silent ceremonial of the setting sun was revealed in all its glowing splendour. In the midst of that stillness the child, all of a sudden, pointed with his finger in front of him and cried: 'Chan-nal Pitty fow.'

Close by on a mud-flat stood a large Kadamba tree in full flower. My lord, the baby, looked at it with greedy eyes, and Raicharan knew his meaning. Only a short time before he had made, out of these very flower balls, a small go-cart; and the child had been so entirely happy dragging it about with a string, that for the whole day Raicharan was not made to put on the reins at all. He was promoted from a horse into a groom.

But Raicharan had no wish that evening to go splashing knee-deep through the mud to reach the flowers. So he quickly pointed his finger in the opposite direction, calling out: 'Oh, look, baby, look! Look at the bird.' And with all sorts of curious noises he pushed the go-cart rapidly away from the tree.

But a child, destined to be a judge, cannot be put off so easily. And besides, there was at the time nothing to attract his eyes. And you cannot keep up for ever the pretence of an imaginary bird.

The little Master's mind was made up, and Raicharan was at his wits' end. 'Very well, baby,' he said at last, 'you sit still in the cart, and I'll go and get you the pretty flower. Only, mind you, don't go near the water.'

As he said this, he made his legs bare to the knee, and waded through the oozing mud towards the tree.

The moment Raicharan had gone, his little Master went off at racing speed to the forbidden water. The baby saw the river rushing by, splashing and gurgling as it went. It seemed as though the disobedient wavelets themselves were running away from some greater Raicharan with the laughter of a thousand children. At the sight of their mischief, the heart of the human child grew excited and restless. He got down stealthily from the go-cart and toddled off towards the river. On his way he picked up a small stick, and leant over the bank of the stream pretending to fish. The mischievous fairies of the river with their mysterious voices seemed inviting him into their play-house.

Raicharan had plucked a handful of flowers from the tree, and was carrying them back in the end of his cloth, with his face wreathed in smiles. But when he reached the go-cart, there was no one there. He looked on all sides and there was no one there. He looked back at the cart and there was no one there.

In that first terrible moment his blood froze within him. Before his eyes the whole universe swam round like a dark mist. From the depth of his broken heart he gave one piercing cry; 'Master, Master, little Master.'

But no voice answered 'Chan-na'. No child laughed mischievously back; no scream of baby delight welcomed his return. Only the river ran on, with its splashing, gurgling noise as before,—as though it knew nothing at all, and had no time to attend to such a tiny human event as the death of a child.

As the evening passed by Raicharan's mistress became very anxious. She sent men out on all sides to search. They went with lanterns in their hands, and reached at last the banks of the Padma. There they found Raicharan rushing up and down the fields, like a stormy wind, shouting the cry of despair: 'Master, Master, little Master!'

When they got Raicharan home at last, he fell prostrate at his mistress's feet. They shook him, and questioned him, and asked him repeatedly where he had left the child; but all he could say was, that he knew nothing.

Though every one held the opinion that the Padma had swallowed the child, there was a lurking doubt left in the mind. For a band of gipsies had been noticed outside the village that afternoon, and some suspicion rested on them. The mother went so far in her wild grief as to think it possible that Raicharan himself had stolen the child. She called him aside with piteous entreaty and said: 'Raicharan, give me back my baby. Oh! give me back my child. Take from me any money you ask, but give me back my child!'

Raicharan only beat his forehead in reply. His mistress ordered him out of the house.

Anukul tried to reason his wife out of this wholly unjust suspicion: 'Why on earth,' he said, 'should he commit such a crime as that?'

The mother only replied: 'The baby had gold ornaments on his body. Who knows?'

It was impossible to reason with her after that.

II

Raicharan went back to his own village. Up to this time he had had no son, and there was no hope that any child would now be born to him. But it came about before the end of a year that his wife gave birth to a son and died.

All overwhelming resentment at first grew up in Raicharan's heart at the sight of this new baby. At the back of his mind was resentful suspicion that it had come as a usurper in place of the little Master. He also thought it would be a grave offence to be happy with a son of his own after what had happened to his master's little child. Indeed, if it had not been for a widowed sister, who mothered the new baby, it would not have lived long.

But a change gradually came over Raicharan's mind. A wonderful thing happened. This new baby in turn began to crawl about, and cross the doorway with mischief in its face. It also showed an amusing cleverness in making its escape to safety. Its voice, its sounds of laughter and tears, its gestures, were those of the little Master. On some days, when Raicharan listened to its crying, his heart suddenly began thumping wildly against his ribs, and it seemed to him that his former little Master was crying somewhere in the unknown land of death because he had lost his Chan-na.

Phailna (for that was the name Raicharan's sister gave to the new baby) soon began to talk. It learnt to say Ba-ba and Ma-ma with a baby accent. When Raicharan heard those familiar sounds the mystery suddenly became clear. The little Master could not cast off the spell of his Chan-na, and therefore he had been reborn in his own house.

The arguments in favour of this were, to Raicharan, altogether beyond dispute:

(i)   The new baby was born soon after his little Master's death.

(ii) His wife could never have accumulated such merit as to give birth to a son in middle age.

(iii) The new baby walked with a toddle and called out

Ba-ba and Ma-ma. There was no sign lacking which marked out the future judge.

Then suddenly Raicharan remembered that terrible accusation of the mother. 'Ah,' he said to himself with amazement, 'the mother's heart was right. She knew I had stolen her child.' When once he had come to this conclusion, he was filled with remorse for his past neglect. He now gave himself over, body and soul, to the new baby, and became its devoted attendant. He began to bring it up, as if it were the son of a rich man. He bought a go-cart, a yellow satin waistcoat, and a gold-embroidered cap. He melted down the ornaments of his dead wife, and made gold bangles and anklets. He refused to let the little child play with any one of the neighbourhood, and became himself its sole companion day and night. As the baby grew up to boyhood, he was so petted and spoilt and clad in such finery that the village children would call him 'Your Lordship', and jeer at him; and older people regarded Raicharan as unaccountably crazy about the child.

At last the time came for the boy to go to school. Raicharan sold his small piece of land, and went to Calcutta. There he got employment with great difficulty as a servant, and sent Phailna to school. He spared no pains to give him the best education, the best clothes, the best food. Meanwhile he lived himself on a mere handful of rice, and would say in secret: 'Ah! my little Master, my dear little

Master, you loved me so much that you came back to my house. You shall never suffer from any neglect of mine.'

Twelve years passed away in this manner. The boy was able to read and write well. He was bright and healthy and good-looking. He paid a great deal of attention to his personal appearance, and was specially careful in parting his hair. He was inclined to extravagance and finery, and spent money freely. He could never quite look on Raicharan as a father, because, though fatherly in affection, he had the manner of a servant. A further fault was this, that Raicharan kept secret from every one that he himself was the father of the child.

The students of the hostel, where Phailna was a boarder, were greatly amused by Raicharan's country manners, and I have to confess that behind his father's back Phailna joined in their fun. But, in the bottom of their hearts, all the students loved the innocent and tender-hearted old man, and Phailna was very fond of him also. But, as I have said before, he loved him with a kind of condescension.

Raicharan grew older and older, and his employer was continually finding fault with him for his incompetent work. He had been starving himself for the boy's sake. So he had grown physically weak, and no longer up to his work. He would forget things, and his mind became dull and stupid. But his employer expected a full servant's work out of him, and would not brook excuses. The money that Raicharan had brought with him from the sale of his land was exhausted. The boy was continually grumbling about his clothes, and asking for more money.

Raicharan made up his mind. He gave up the situation where he was working as a servant, and left some money with Phailna and said: 'I have some business to do at home in my village, and shall be back soon.'

He went off at once to Baraset where Anukul was magistrate. Anukul's wife was still broken down with grief. She had had no other child.

One day Anukul was resting after a long and weary day in court. His wife was buying, at an exorbitant price, a herb from a mendicant quack, which was said to ensure the birth of a child. A voice of greeting was heard in the courtyard. Anukul went out to see who was there. It was Raicharan. Anukul's heart was softened when he saw his old servant. He asked him many questions, and offered to take him back into service.

Raicharan smiled faintly, and said in reply, 'I want to make obeisance to my mistress.'

Anukul went with Raicharan into the house, where the mistress did not receive him as warmly as his old master. Raicharan took no notice of this, but folded his hands, and said: 'It was not the Padma that stole your baby. It was I.'

Anukul exclaimed: 'Great God! Eh! What! Where is he?' Raicharan replied: 'He is with me, I will bring him the day after to-morrow.'

It was Sunday. There was no magistrate's court sitting. Both husband and wife were looking expectantly along the road, waiting from early morning for Raicharan's appearance. At ten o'clock he came, leading Phailna by the hand.

Anukul's wife, without a question, took the boy into her lap, and was wild with excitement, sometimes laughing, sometimes weeping, touching him, kissing his hair and his forehead, and gazing into his face with hungry, eager eyes. The boy was very good-looking and dressed like a gentleman's son. The heart of Anukul brimmed over with a sudden rush of affection.

Nevertheless the magistrate in him asked: 'Have you any proofs?' Raicharan said: 'How could there be any proof of such a deed? God alone knows that I stole your boy, and no one else in the world.'

When Anukul saw how eagerly his wife was clinging to the boy, he realized the futility of asking for proofs. It would be wiser to believe. And then—where could an old man like Raicharan get such a boy from? And why should his faithful servant deceive him for nothing?

'But,' he added severely, 'Raicharan, you must not stay here.'

'Where shall I go, Master?' said Raicharan, in a choking voice, folding his hands, 'I am old. Who will take in an old man as a servant?'

The mistress said: 'Let him stay. My child will be pleased. I forgive him.'

But Anukul's magisterial conscience would not allow him. 'No,' he said, 'he cannot be forgiven for what he has done.'

Raicharan bowed to the ground, and clasped Anukul's feet. 'Master,' he cried, 'let me stay. It was not I who did it. It was God.'

Anukul's conscience was worse stricken than ever, when Raicharan tried to put the blame on God's shoulders.

'No,' he said, 'I could not allow it. I cannot trust you any more. You have done an act of treachery.'

Raicharan rose to his feet and said: 'It was not I who did it.'

'Who was it then?' asked Anukul.

Raicharan replied: 'It was my fate.'

But no educated man could take this for an excuse. Anukul remained obdurate.

When Phailna saw that he was the wealthy magistrate's son, and not Raicharan's, he was angry at first, thinking that he had been cheated all this time of his birthright. But seeing Raicharan in distress, he generously said to his father: 'Father, forgive him. Even if you don't let him live with us, let him have a small monthly pension.'

After hearing this, Raicharan did not utter another word. He looked for the last time on the face of his son; he made obeisance to his old master and mistress. Then he went out, and was mingled with the numberless people of the world.

At the end of the month Anukul sent him some money to his village. But the money came back. There was no one there of the name of Raicharan.

the parrot's training

Once upon a time there was a bird. It was ignorant. It sang all right, but never recited scriptures. It hopped pretty frequently, but lacked manners.

Said the Raja to himself: 'Ignorance is costly in the long run. For fools consume as much food as their betters, and yet give nothing in return.'

He called his nephews to his presence and told them that the bird must have a sound schooling.

The pundits were summoned, and at once went to the root of the matter.

They decided that the ignorance of birds was due to their natural habit of living in poor nests. Therefore, according to the pundits, the first thing necessary for this bird's education was a suitable cage.

The pundits had their rewards and went home happy.

A golden cage was built with gorgeous decorations. Crowds came to see it from all parts of the world. 'Culture, captured and caged!' exclaimed some, in a rapture of ecstasy, and burst into tears. Others remarked: 'Even if culture be missed, the cage will remain, to the end, a substantial fact. How fortunate for the bird!'

The goldsmith filled his bag with money and lost no time in sailing homewards.

The pundit sat down to educate the bird. With proper deliberation he took his pinch of snuff, as he said: 'Textbooks can never be too many for our purpose!'

The nephews brought together an enormous crowd of scribes. They copied from books, and copied from copies, till the manuscripts were piled up to an unreachable height. Men murmured in amazement: 'Oh, the tower of culture, egregiously high! The end of it lost in the clouds!'

The scribes, with light hearts, hurried home, their pockets heavily laden.

The nephews were furiously busy keeping the cage in proper trim. As their constant scrubbing and polishing went on, the people said with satisfaction: 'This is progress indeed!'

Men were employed in large numbers, and supervisors were still more numerous. These, with their cousins of all different degrees of distance, built a palace for themselves and lived there happily ever after.

Whatever may be its other deficiencies, the world is never in want of fault-finders; and they went about saying that every creature remotely connected with the cage flourished beyond words, excepting only the bird.

When this remark reached the Raja's ears, he summoned his nephews before him and said: 'My dear nephews, what is this that we hear?'

The nephews said in answer: 'Sire, let the testimony of the goldsmiths and the pundits, the scribes and the supervisors, be taken, if the truth is to be known. Food is scarce with the fault-finders, and that is why their tongues have gained in sharpness.'

The explanation was so luminously satisfactory that the Raja decorated each one of his nephews with his own rare jewels.

The Raja at length, being desirous of seeing with his own eyes how his Education Department busied itself with the little bird, made his appearance one day at the great Hall of Learning.

From the gate rose the sounds of conch-shells and gongs, horns, bugles and trumpets, cymbals, drums and kettle-drums, tomtoms, tambourines, flutes, fifes, barrel-organs and bagpipes. The pundits began chanting mantras with their topmost voices, while the goldsmiths, scribes, supervisors, and their numberless cousins of all different degrees of distance, loudly raised a round of cheers.

The nephews smiled and said: 'Sire, what do you think of it all?'

The Raja said: 'It does seem so fearfully like a sound principle of Education!'

Mightily pleased, the Raja was about to remount his elephant, when the fault-finder, from behind some bush, cried out: 'Maharaja, have you seen the bird?'

'Indeed, I have not!' exclaimed the Raja, 'I completely forgot about the bird.'

Turning back, he asked the pundits about the method they followed in instructing the bird. It was shown to him. He was immensely impressed. The method was so stupendous that the bird looked ridiculously unimportant in comparison. The Raja was satisfied that there was no flaw in the arrangements. As for any complaint from the bird itself, that simply could not be expected. Its throat was so completely choked with the leaves from the books that it could neither whistle nor whisper. It sent a thrill through one's body to watch the process.

This time, while remounting his elephant, the Raja ordered his State ear-puller to give a thoroughly good pull at both the ears of the fault-finder.

The bird thus crawled on, duly and properly, to the safest verge of inanity. In fact, its progress was satisfactory in the extreme. Nevertheless, nature occasionally triumphed over training, and when the morning light peeped into the bird's cage it sometimes fluttered its wings in a reprehensible manner. And, though it is hard to believe, it pitifully pecked at its bars with its feeble beak.

'What impertinence!' growled the kotwal.

The blacksmith, with his forge and hammer, took his place in the Raja's Department of Education. Oh, what resounding blows! The iron chain was soon completed, and the bird's wings were clipped.

The Raja's brothers-in-law looked back, and shook their heads, saying: 'These birds not only lack good sense, but also gratitude!'

With textbook in one hand and baton in the other, the pundits gave the poor bird what may fitly be called lessons!

The kotwal was honoured with a title for his watchfulness, and the blacksmith for his skill in forging chains.

The bird died.

Nobody had the least notion how long ago this had happened. The fault-finder was the first man to spread the rumour.

The Raja called his nephews and asked them. 'My dear nephews, what is this that we hear?'

The nephews said: 'Sire, the bird's education has been completed.'

'Does it hop?' the Raja enquired.

'Never!' said the nephews.

'Does it fly?'

'No.'

'Bring me the bird,' said the Raja.

The bird was brought to him, guarded by the kotwal and

the sepoys and the sowars. The Raja poked its body with his finger. Only its inner stuffing of book-leaves rustled.

Outside the window, the murmur of the spring breeze amongst the newly budded asoka leaves made the April morning wistful.

the home-coming

Phatik Chakravorti was ringleader among the boys of the village. A new mischief got into his head. There was a heavy log lying on the mud-flat of the river waiting to be shaped into a mast for a boat. He decided that they should all work together to shift the log by main force from its place and roll it away. The owner of the log would be angry and surprised, and they would all enjoy the fun. Every one seconded the proposal, and it was carried unanimously.

But just as the fun was about to begin, Makhan, Phatik's younger brother, sauntered up and sat down on the log in front of them all without a word. The boys were puzzled for a moment. He was pushed, rather timidly, by one of the boys and told to get up; but he remained quite unconcerned. He appeared like a young philosopher meditating on the futility of games. Phatik was furious. 'Makhan,' he cried, 'if you don't get down this minute I'll thrash you!'

Makhan only moved to a more comfortable position.

Now, if Phatik was to keep his regal dignity before the public, it was clear he ought to carry out his threat. But his courage failed him at the crisis. His fertile brain, however, rapidly seized upon a new manœuvre which would discomfit his brother and afford his followers an added amusement. He gave the word of command to roll the log and Makhan over together. Makhan heard the order and made it a point of honour to stick on. But he overlooked the fact, like those who attempt earthly fame in other matters, that there was peril in it.

The boys began to heave at the log with all their might, calling out, 'One, two, three, go!' At the word 'go' the log went; and with it went Makhan's philosophy, glory and all.

The other boys shouted themselves hoarse with delight. But Phatik was a little frightened. He knew what was coming. And, sure enough, Makhan rose from Mother Earth blind as Fate and screaming like the Furies. He rushed at Phatik and scratched his face and beat him and kicked him, and then went crying home. The first act of the drama was over.

Phatik wiped his face, and sat down on the edge of a sunken barge by the river bank, and began to chew a piece of grass. A boat came up to the landing and a middle-aged man, with grey hair and dark moustache, stepped on shore. He saw the boy sitting there doing nothing and asked him where the Chakravortis lived. Phatik went on chewing the grass and said: 'Over there,' but it was quite impossible to tell where he pointed. The stranger asked him again. He swung his legs to and fro on the side of the barge and said: 'Go and find out,' and continued to chew the grass as before.

But now a servant came down from the house and told Phatik his mother wanted him. Phatik refused to move. But the servant was the master on this occasion. He took Phatik up roughly and carried him, kicking and struggling in impotent rage.

When Phatik came into the house, his mother saw him. She called out angrily: 'So you have been hitting Makhan again?'

Phatik answered indignantly: 'No, I haven't! Who told you that?'

His mother shouted: 'Don't tell lies! You have.'

Phatik said sullenly: 'I tell you, I haven't. You ask Makhan!' But Makhan thought it best to stick to his previous statement. He said: 'Yes, mother. Phatik did hit me.'

Phatik's patience was already exhausted. He could not bear this injustice. He rushed at Makhan and hammered him with blows: 'Take that,' he cried, 'and that, and that, for telling lies.'

His mother took Makhan's side in a moment, and pulled Phatik away, beating him with her hands. When Phatik pushed her aside, she shouted out: 'What! you little villain! Would you hit your own mother?'

It was just at this critical juncture that the grey-haired stranger arrived. He asked what was the matter. Phatik looked sheepish and ashamed.

But when his mother stepped back and looked at the stranger, her anger was changed to surprise. For she recognized her brother and cried: 'Why, Dada! Where have you come from?'

As she said these words, she bowed to the ground and touched his feet. Her brother had gone away soon after she had married; and he had started business in Bombay. His sister had lost her husband while he was there. Bishamber had now come back to Calcutta and had at once made enquiries about his sister. He had then hastened to see her as soon as he found out where she was.

The next few days were full of rejoicing. The brother asked after the education of the two boys. He was told by his sister that Phatik was a perpetual nuisance. He was lazy, disobedient, and wild. But Makhan was as good as gold, as quiet as a lamb, and very fond of reading. Bishamber kindly offered to take Phatik off his sister's hands and educate him with his own children in Calcutta. The widowed mother readily agreed. When his uncle asked Phatik if he would like to go to Calcutta with him, his joy knew no bounds and he said: 'Oh, yes, uncle!' in a way that made it quite clear that he meant it.

It was an immense relief to the mother to get rid of Phatik. She had a prejudice against the boy, and no love was lost between the two brothers. She was in daily fear that he would either drown Makhan some day in the river, or break his head in a fight, or run him into some danger.

At the same time she was a little distressed to see Phatik's extreme eagerness to get away.

Phatik, as soon as all was settled, kept asking his uncle every minute when they were to start. He was on pins and needles all day long with excitement and lay awake most of the night. He bequeathed to Makhan, in perpetuity, his fishing-rod, his big kite, and his marbles. Indeed, at this time of departure, his generosity towards Makhan was unbounded.

When they reached Calcutta, Phatik made the acquaintance of his aunt for the first time. She was by no means pleased with this unnecessary addition to her family. She found her own three boys quite enough to manage without taking any one else. And to bring a village lad of fourteen into their midst was terribly upsetting. Bishamber should really have thought twice before committing such an indiscretion.

In this world of human affairs there is no worse nuisance than a boy at the age of fourteen. He is neither ornamental nor useful. It is impossible to shower affection on him as on a little boy; and he is always getting in the way. If he talks with a childish lisp he is called a baby, and if he answers in a grown-up way he is called impertinent. In fact any talk at all from him is resented. Then he is at the unattractive, growing age. He grows out of his clothes with indecent haste; his voice grows hoarse and breaks and quavers; his face grows suddenly angular and unsightly. It is easy to excuse the shortcomings of early childhood, but it is hard to tolerate even unavoidable lapses in a boy of fourteen. The lad himself becomes painfully self-conscious. When he talks with elderly people he is either unduly forward, or else so unduly shy that he appears ashamed of his very existence.

Yet it is at this very age when, in his heart of hearts, a young lad most craves for recognition and love; and he becomes the devoted slave of any one who shows him consideration. But none dare openly love him, for that would be regarded as undue indulgence and therefore bad for the boy. So, what with scolding and chiding, he becomes very much like a stray dog that has lost his master.

For a boy of fourteen his own home is the only Paradise. To live in a strange house with strange people is little short of torture, while the height of bliss is to receive the kind looks of women and never to be slighted by them.

It was anguish to Phatik to be the unwelcome guest in his aunt's house, despised by this elderly woman and slighted on every occasion. If ever she asked him to do anything for her, he would be so overjoyed that he would overdo it; and then she would tell him not to be so stupid, but to get on with his lessons.

The cramped atmosphere of neglect oppressed Phatik so much that he felt that he could hardly breathe. He wanted to go out into the open country and fill his lungs with fresh air. But there was no open country to go to. Surrounded on all sides by Calcutta houses and walls, he would dream night after night of his village home and long to be back there. He remembered the glorious meadow where he used to fly his kite all day long; the broad river-banks where he would wander about the live-long day singing and shouting for joy; the narrow brook where he could go and dive and swim at any time he liked. He thought of his band of boy companions over whom he was despot; and, above all, the memory of that tyrant mother of his, who had such a prejudice against him, occupied him day and night. A kind of physical love like that of animals, a longing to be in the presence of the one who is loved, an inexpressible wistfulness during absence, a silent cry of the inmost heart for the mother, like the lowing of a calf in the twilight,—this love, which was almost an animal instinct, agitated the shy, nervous, lean, uncouth and ugly boy. No one could understand it, but it preyed upon his mind continually.

There was no more backward boy in the whole school than Phatik. He gaped and remained silent when the teacher asked him a question, and like an overladen ass patiently suffered all the blows that came down on his back. When other boys were out at play, he stood wistfully by the window and gazed at the roofs of the distant houses. And if by chance he espied children playing on the open terrace of any roof, his heart would ache with longing.

One day he summoned up all his courage and asked his uncle: 'Uncle, when can I go home?'

His uncle answered: 'Wait till the holidays come.'

But the holidays would not come till October and there was a long time still to wait.

One day Phatik lost his lesson book. Even with the help of books he had found it very difficult indeed to prepare his lesson. Now it was impossible. Day after day the teacher would cane him unmercifully. His condition became so abjectly miserable that even his cousins were ashamed to own him. They began to jeer and insult him more than the other boys. He went to his aunt at last and told her that he had lost his book.

His aunt pursed her lips in contempt and said: 'You great clumsy, country lout! How can I afford, with all my family, to buy you new books five times a month?'

That night, on his way back from school, Phatik had a bad headache with a fit of shivering. He felt he was going to have an attack of malarial fever. His one great fear was that he would be a nuisance to his aunt.

The next morning Phatik was nowhere to be seen. All searches in the neighbourhood proved futile. The rain had been pouring in torrents all night, and those who went out in search of the boy got drenched through to the skin. At last Bishamber asked help from the police.

At the end of the day a police van stopped at the door before the house. It was still raining and the streets were all flooded. Two constables brought out Phatik in their arms and placed him before Bishamber. He was wet through from head to foot, muddy all over, his face and eyes flushed red with fever and his limbs trembling. Bishamber carried him in his arms and took him into the inner apartments. When his wife saw him she exclaimed: 'What a heap of trouble this boy has given us! Hadn't you better send him home?'

Phatik heard her words and sobbed out loud: 'Uncle, I was just going home; but they dragged me back again.'

The fever rose very high, and all that night the boy was delirious. Bishamber brought in a doctor. Phatik opened his eyes, flushed with fever, and looked up to the ceiling and said vacantly: 'Uncle, have the holidays come yet?'

Bishamber wiped the tears from his own eyes and took Phatik's lean and burning hands in his own and sat by him through the night. The boy began again to mutter. At last his voice became excited: 'Mother!' he cried, 'don't beat me like that.... Mother! I *am* telling the truth!'

The next day Phatik became conscious for a short time. He turned his eyes about the room, as if expecting some one to come. At last, with an air of disappointment, his head sank back on the pillow. He turned his face to the wall with a deep sigh.

Bishamber knew his thoughts and bending down his head whispered: 'Phatik, I have sent for your mother.'

The day went by. The doctor said in a troubled voice that the boy's condition was very critical.

Phatik began to cry out: 'By the mark—three fathoms. By the mark—four fathoms. By the mark—.' He had heard the sailor on the river-steamer calling out the mark on the plumb-line. Now he was himself plumbing an unfathomable sea.

Later in the day Phatik's mother burst into the room, like a whirlwind, and began to toss from side to side and moan and cry in a loud voice.

Bishamber tried to calm her agitation, but she flung herself on the bed, and cried: 'Phatik, my darling, my darling.'

Phatik stopped his restless movements for a moment. His hands ceased beating up and down. He said: 'Eh?'

The mother cried again: 'Phatik, my darling, my darling.'

Phatik very slowly turned his head and without seeing anybody said: 'Mother, the holidays have come.'

master mashai

I

Adhar Babu lives upon the interest of the capital left him by his father. Only the brokers, negotiating loans, come to his drawing room and smoke the silver-chased hookah, and the clerks from the attorney's office discuss the terms of some mortgage or the amount of the stamp fees. He is so careful with his money that even the most dogged efforts of the boys from the local football club fail to make any impression on his pocket.

At the time this story opens a new guest came into his household. After a long period of despair, his wife, Nanibala, bore him a son.

The child resembled his mother—large eyes, well-formed nose, and fair complexion. Ratikanta, Adharlal's protégé, gave verdict, 'He is worthy of this noble house.' They named him Venugopal.

Never before had Adharlal's wife expressed any opinion differing from her husband's on household expenses.

There had been a hot discussion now and then about the propriety of some necessary item and up to this time she had merely acknowledged defeat with silent contempt. But now Adharlal could no longer maintain his supremacy. He had to give way little by little when things for his son were in question.

II

As Venugopal grew up, his father gradually became accustomed to spending money on him. He obtained an old teacher, who had a considerable repute for his learning and also for his success in dragging impassable boys through their examinations. But such a training does not lead to the cultivation of amiability. This man tried his best to win the boy's heart, but the little that was left in him of the natural milk of human kindness had turned sour, and the child repulsed his advances from the very beginning. The mother, in consequence, objected to him strongly, and complained that the very sight of him made her boy ill. So the teacher left.

Just then, Haralal made his appearance with a dirty dress and a torn pair of old canvas shoes. Haralal's mother, who was a widow, had kept him with great difficulty at a District school out of the scanty earnings which she made by cooking in strange houses and husking rice. He managed to pass the Matriculation and determined to go to College. As a result of his half-starved condition, his pinched face tapered to a point in an unnatural manner—like Cape Comorin in the map of India; and the only broad portion of it was his forehead, which resembled the ranges of the Himalayas.

The servant asked Haralal what he wanted, and he answered timidly that he wished to see the master.

The servant answered sharply: 'You can't see him.' Haralal was hesitating, at a loss what to do next, when Venugopal, who had finished his game in the garden, suddenly came to the door. The servant shouted at Haralal: 'Get away.' Quite unaccountably Venugopal grew excited and cried: 'No, he shan't get away.' And he dragged the stranger to his father.

Adharlal had just risen from his midday sleep and was sitting quietly on the upper verandah in his cane chair, rocking his legs. Ratikanta was enjoying his hookah, seated in a chair next to him. He asked Haralal how far he had got in his reading. The young man bent his head and answered that he had passed the Matriculation. Ratikanta looked stern and expressed surprise that he should be so backward for his age. Haralal kept silence. It was Ratikanta's special pleasure to torture his patron's dependants, whether actual or potential.

Suddenly it struck Adharlal that he would be able to employ this youth as a tutor for his son on next to nothing. He agreed, there and then, to take him at a salary of five rupees a month with board and lodging free.

III

This time the post of tutor remained occupied longer than before. From the very beginning of their acquaintance Haralal and his pupil became great friends. Never before did Haralal have such an opportunity of loving any young human creature. His mother had been so poor and dependent, that he had never had the privilege of playing with the children where she was employed at work. He had not hitherto suspected the hidden stores of love which lay all the while accumulating in his own heart.

Venu, also, was glad to find a companion in Haralal. He was the only boy in the house. His two younger sisters were looked down upon, as unworthy of being his playmates. So his new tutor became his only companion, patiently bearing the undivided weight of the tyranny of his child friend.

IV

Venu was now eleven. Haralal had passed his Intermediate, winning a scholarship. He was working hard for his B.A. degree. After College lectures were over, he would take Venu out into the public park and tell him stories about the heroes from Greek History and Victor Hugo's romances. The child used to get quite impatient to run to Haralal, after school hours, in spite of his mother's attempts to keep him by her side.

This displeased Nanibala. She thought that it was a deep-laid plot of Haralal's to captivate her boy, in order to prolong his own appointment. One day she talked to him from behind the purdah: 'It is your duty to teach my son only for an hour or two in the morning and evening. But why are you always with him? The child has nearly forgotten his own parents. You must understand that a man of your position is no fit companion for a boy belonging to this house.'

Haralal's voice choked a little as he answered that for the future he would merely be Venu's teacher and would keep away from him at other times.

It was Haralal's usual practice to begin his College study early before dawn. The child would come to him directly after he had washed himself. There was a small pool in the garden and they used to feed the fish in it with puffed rice. Venu was also engaged in building a miniature garden-house, at the corner of the garden, with its liliputian gates and hedges and gravel paths. When the sun became too hot they would go back into the house, and Venu would have his morning lesson from Haralal.

On the day in question Venu had risen earlier than usual, because he wished to hear the end of the story which Haralal had begun the evening before. But he found his teacher absent. When asked about him, the door-servant said that he had gone out. At lesson time Venu remained unnaturally quiet. He never even asked Haralal why he had gone out, but went on mechanically with his lessons. When the child was with his mother taking his breakfast, she asked him what had happened to make him so gloomy, and why he was not eating his food. Venu gave no answer. After his meal his mother caressed him and questioned him repeatedly. Venu burst out crying and said, 'Master Mashai.' His mother asked Venu, 'What about Master Mashai?' But Venu found it difficult to name the offence which his teacher had committed.

His mother said to Venu: 'Has your Master Mashai been saying anything to you against *me?*'

Venu could not understand the question and went away.

V

There was a theft in Adhar Babu's house. The police were called in to investigate. Even Haralal's trunks were searched. Ratikanta said with meaning: 'The man who steals anything, does not keep his thefts in his own box.'

Adharlal called his son's tutor and said to him: 'It will not be convenient for me to keep any of you in my own house. From to-day you will have to take up your quarters outside, only coming in to teach my son at the proper time.'

Ratikanta said sagely, drawing at his hookah: 'That is a good proposal—good for both parties.'

Haralal did not utter a word, but he sent a letter saying that it would be no longer possible for him to remain as tutor to Venu.

When Venu came back from school, he found his tutor's room empty. Even that broken steel trunk of his was absent. The rope was stretched across the corner, but there were no clothes or towel hanging on it. Only on the table, which formerly was strewn with books and papers, stood a bowl containing some gold-fish with a label on which was written the word 'Venu' in Haralal's handwriting. The boy ran up at once to his father and asked him what had happened. His father told him that Haralal had resigned his post. Venu went to his room and flung himself down and began to cry. Adharlal did not know what to do with him.

The next day, when Haralal was sitting on his wooden bedstead in the Hostel, debating with himself whether he should attend his college lectures, suddenly he saw Adhar Babu's servant coming into his room followed by Venu. Venu at once ran up to him and threw his arms round his neck asking him to come back to the house.

Haralal could not explain why it was absolutely impossible for him to go back, but the memory of those clinging arms and that pathetic request used to choke his breath with emotion long after.

VI

Haralal found out, after this, that his mind was in an unsettled state, and that he had but a small chance of winning the scholarship, even if he could pass the examination. At the same time, he knew that, without the scholarship, he could not continue his studies. So he tried to get employment in some office.

Fortunately for him, an English Manager of a big merchant firm took a fancy to him at first sight. After only a brief exchange of words the Manager asked him if he had any experience, and could he bring any testimonial. Haralal could only answer 'No'; nevertheless a post was offered him of twenty rupees a month and fifteen rupees were allowed him in advance to help him to come properly dressed to the office.

The Manager made Haralal work extremely hard. He had to stay on after office hours and sometimes go to his master's house late in the evening. But, in this way, he learnt his work quicker than others, and his fellow clerks became jealous of him and tried to injure him, but without effect. He rented a small house in a narrow lane and brought his mother to live with him as soon as his salary was raised to forty rupees a month. Thus happiness came back to his mother after weary years of waiting.

Haralal's mother used to express a desire to see Venugopal, of whom she had heard so much. She wished to prepare some dishes with her own hand and to ask him to come just once to dine with her son. Haralal avoided the subject by saying that his house was not big enough to invite him for that purpose.

VII

The news reached Haralal that Venu's mother had died. He could not wait a moment, but went at once to Adharlal's house to see Venu. After that they began to see each other frequently.

But times had changed. Venu, stroking his budding moustache, had grown quite a young man of fashion. Friends, befitting his present condition, were numerous. That old dilapidated study chair and ink-stained desk had vanished, and the room now seemed to be bursting with pride at its new acquisitions—its looking-glasses, oleographs, and other furniture. Venu had entered college, but showed no haste in crossing the boundary of the Intermediate examination.

Haralal remembered his mother's request to invite Venu to dinner. After great hesitation, he did so. Venugopal, with his handsome face, at once won the mother's heart. But as soon as ever the meal was over he became impatient to go, and looking at his gold watch he explained that he had pressing engagements elsewhere. Then he jumped into his carriage, which was waiting at the door, and drove away. Haralal with a sigh said to himself that he would never invite him again.

VIII

One day, on returning from office, Haralal noticed the presence of a man in the dark room on the ground floor of his house. Possibly he would have passed him by, had not the heavy scent of some foreign perfume attracted his attention. Haralal asked who was there, and the answer came:

'It is I, Master Mashai.'

'What is the matter, Venu?' said Haralal. 'When did you arrive?'

'I came hours ago,' said Venu. 'I did not know that you returned so late.'

They went upstairs together and Haralal lighted the lamp and asked Venu whether all was well. Venu replied that his college classes were becoming a fearful bore, and his father did not realize how dreadfully hard it was for him to go on in the same class, year after year, with students much younger than himself. Haralal asked him what he wished to do. Venu then told him that he wanted to go to England and become a barrister. He gave an instance of a student, much less advanced than himself, who was getting ready to go. Haralal asked him if he had received his father's permission. Venu replied that his father would not hear a word of it until he had passed the Intermediate, and that was an impossibility in his present frame of mind. Haralal suggested that he himself should go and try to talk over his father.

'No,' said Venu, 'I can never allow that!'

Haralal asked Venu to stay for dinner and while they were waiting he gently placed his hand on Venu's shoulder and said:

'Venu, you should not quarrel with your father, or leave home.'

Venu jumped up angrily and said that if he was not welcome, he could go elsewhere. Haralal caught him by the hand and implored him not to go away without taking his food. But Venu snatched away his hand and was just leaving the room when Haralal's mother brought the food in on a tray. On seeing Venu about to leave she pressed him to remain and he did so with bad grace.

While he was eating, the sound of a carriage stopping at the door was heard. First a servant entered the room with creaking shoes and then Adhar Babu himself. Venu's face became pale. The mother left the room as soon as she saw strangers enter. Adhar Babu called out to Haralal in a voice thick with anger:

'Ratikanta gave me full warning, but I could not believe that you had such devilish cunning hidden in you. So, you think you're going to live upon Venu? This is sheer kidnapping, and I shall prosecute you in the Police Court.'

Venu silently followed his father and went out of the house.

IX

The firm to which Haralal belonged began to buy up large quantities of rice and dhal from the country districts. To pay for this, Haralal had to take the cash every Saturday morning by the early train and disburse it. There were special centres where the brokers and middlemen would come with their receipts and accounts for settlement. Some discussion had taken place in the office about Haralal being entrusted with this work, without any security, but the Manager undertook all the responsibility and said that a security was not needed. This special work used to go on from the middle of December to the middle of April. Haralal would get back from it very late at night.

One day, after his return, he was told by his mother that Venu had called and that she had persuaded him to take his dinner at their house. This happened more than once. The mother said that it was because Venu missed his own mother, and the tears came into her eyes as she spoke about it.

One day Venu waited for Haralal to return and had a long talk with him.

'Master Mashai!' he said. 'Father has become so cantankerous of late that I cannot live with him any longer. And, besides, I know that he is getting ready to marry again. Ratikanta is seeking a suitable match, and they are always conspiring about it. There used to be a time when my father would get anxious if I were absent from home even for a few hours. Now, if I am away for more than a week, he takes no notice—indeed he is greatly relieved. If this marriage takes place, I feel that I cannot live in the house any longer. You must show me a way out of this. I want to become independent.'

Haralal felt deeply pained, but he did not know how to help his former pupil. Venu said that he was determined to go to England and become a barrister. Somehow or other he must get the passage money out of his father: he could borrow it on a note of hand and his father would have to pay when the creditors filed a suit. With this borrowed money he would get away, and when he was in England his father was certain to remit his expenses.

'But who is there,' Haralal asked, 'who would advance you the money?'

'You!' said Venu.

'I!' exclaimed Haralal in amazement.

'Yes,' said Venu, 'I've seen the servant bringing heaps of money here in bags.'

'The servant and the money belong to someone else.'

Haralal explained why the money came to his house at night, like birds to their nest, to be scattered next morning.

'But can't the Manager advance the sum?' Venu asked.

'He may do so,' said Haralal, 'if your father stands security.'

The discussion ended at this point.

X

One Friday night a carriage and pair stopped before Haralal's lodging house. When Venu was announced Haralal was counting money in his bedroom, seated on the floor. Venu entered the room dressed in a strange manner. He had discarded his Bengali dress and was wearing a Parsee coat and trousers and had a cap on his head. Rings were prominent on almost all the fingers of both hands, and a thick gold chain was hanging round his neck; there was a gold-watch in his pocket, and diamond studs could be seen peeping from his shirt sleeves. Haralal at once asked him what was the matter and why he was wearing that dress.

'My father's marriage,' said Venu, 'comes off to-morrow. He tried hard to keep it from me, but I found it out. I asked him to allow me to go to our garden-house at Barrackpur for a few days, and he was only too glad to get rid of me so easily. I am going there, and I wish to God I had never to come back.'

Haralal looked pointedly at the rings on his fingers. Venu explained that they had belonged to his mother. Haralal then asked him if he had already had his dinner. He answered, 'Yes, haven't you had yours?'

'No,' said Haralal, 'I cannot leave this room until I have all the money safely locked up in this iron chest.'

'Go and take your dinner,' said Venu, 'while I keep guard here: your mother will be waiting for you.'

For a moment Haralal hesitated, and then he went out and had his dinner. In a short time he came back with his mother and the three of them sat among the bags of money talking together. When it was about midnight, Venu took out his watch and looked at it and jumped up saying that he would miss his train. Then he asked Haralal to keep all his rings and his watch and chain until he asked for them again. Haralal put them all together in a leather bag and laid it in the iron safe. Venu went out.

The canvas bags containing the currency notes had already been placed in the safe: only the loose coins remained to be counted over and put away with the rest.

XI

Haralal lay down on the floor of the same room, with the key under his pillow, and went to sleep. He dreamt that Venu's mother was loudly reproaching him from behind the curtain. Her words were indistinct, but rays of different colours from the jewels on her body kept piercing the curtain like needles and violently vibrating. Haralal struggled to call Venu, but his voice seemed to forsake him. At last, with a noise, the curtain fell down. Haralal started up from his sleep and found darkness piled up round about him. A sudden gust of wind had flung open the window and put out the light. Haralal's whole body was wet with perspiration. He relighted the lamp and saw, by the clock, that it was four in the morning. There was no time to sleep again; for he had to get ready to start.

After Haralal had washed his face and hands, his mother called from her own room, 'Baba, why are you up so soon?'

It was the habit of Haralal to see his mother's face the first thing in the morning in order to bring a blessing upon the day. His mother said to him: 'I was dreaming that you were going out to bring back a bride for yourself.' Haralal went to his own bedroom and began to take out the bags containing the silver and the currency notes.

Suddenly his heart stopped beating. Three of the bags appeared to be empty. He knocked them against the iron safe, but this only proved his fear to be true. He opened them and shook them with all his might. Two letters from Venu dropped out from one of the bags. One was addressed to his father and one to Haralal.

Haralal tore open his own letter and began reading. The words seemed to run into one another. He trimmed the lamp, but felt as if he could not understand what he read. Yet the purport of the letter was clear. Venu had taken three thousand rupees, in currency notes, and had started for England. The steamer was to sail before day-break that very morning. The letter ended with the words: 'I am explaining everything in a letter to my father. He will pay off the debt; and then, again, my mother's ornaments, which I have left in your care, will more than cover the amount I have taken.'

Haralal locked up his room and hired a carriage and went with all haste to the jetty. But he did not know even the name of the steamer which Venu had taken. He ran the whole length of the wharves from Prinsep's Ghat to Metiaburuj. He found that two steamers had started on their voyage to England early that morning. It was impossible for him to know which of them carried Venu, or how to reach him.

When Haralal got home, the sun was strong and the whole of Calcutta was awake. Everything before his eyes seemed blurred. He felt as if he were pushing against a fearful obstacle which was bodiless and without pity. His mother came on the verandah to ask him anxiously where he had gone. With a dry laugh he said to her, 'To bring home a bride for myself,' and then he fainted away.

On opening his eyes after a while, Haralal asked his mother to leave him. Entering his room, he shut the door from the inside while his mother remained seated on the floor of the verandah in the fierce glare of the sun. She kept calling to him fitfully, almost mechanically, 'Baba, Baba!'

The servant came from the Manager's office and knocked at the door, saying that they would miss the train if they did not start out at once. Haralal called from inside, 'It will not be possible for me to start this morning.'

'Then where are we to go, sir?'

'I will tell you later on.'

The servant went downstairs with a gesture of impatience.

Suddenly Haralal thought of the ornaments which Venu had left behind. Up till now he had completely forgotten about them, but with the thought came instant relief. He took the leather bag containing them, and also Venu's letter to his father, and left the house.

Before he reached Adharlal's house he could hear the bands playing for the wedding, yet on entering he could feel that there had been some disturbance. Haralal was told that there had been a theft the night before and one or two servants were suspected. Adhar Babu was sitting in the upper verandah flushed with anger and Ratikanta was smoking his hookah. Haralal said to Adhar Babu, 'I have something private to tell you.' Adharlal flared up, 'I have no time now!' He was afraid that Haralal had come to borrow money or to ask his help. Ratikanta suggested that if there was any delicacy in making the request in his presence he would leave the place. Adharlal told him angrily to sit where he was. Then Haralal handed over the bag which Venu had left behind. Adharlal asked what was inside it and Haralal opened it and gave the contents into his hands.

Then Adhar Babu said with a sneer: 'It's a paying business that you two have started—you and your former pupil! You were certain that the stolen property would be traced, and so you come along with it to me to claim a reward!'

Haralal presented the letter which Venu had written to his father. This only made Adharlal all the more furious.

'What's all this?' he shouted, 'I'll call for the police! My son has not yet come of age—and *you* have smuggled him out of the country! I'll bet my soul you've lent him a few hundred rupees, and then taken a note of hand for three thousand! But I am not going to be bound by *this*!'

'I never advanced him any money at all,' said Haralal.

'Then how did he find it?' said Adharlal, 'Do you mean to tell me he broke open your safe and stole it?'

Haralal stood silent.

Ratikanta sarcastically remarked: 'I don't believe this fellow ever set hands on as much as three thousand rupees in his life.'

When Haralal left the house he seemed to have lost the power of dreading anything, or even of being anxious. His mind seemed to refuse to work. Directly he entered the lane he saw a carriage waiting before his own lodging. For a moment he felt certain that it was Venu's. It was impossible to believe that his calamity could be so hopelessly final.

Haralal went up quickly, but found an English assistant from the firm sitting inside the carriage. The man came out when he saw Haralal and took him by the hand and asked him: 'Why didn't you go out by train this morning?' The servant had told the Manager his suspicions and he had sent this man to find out.

Haralal answered: 'Notes to the amount of three thousand rupees are missing.'

The man asked how that could have happened.

Haralal remained silent.

The man said to Haralal: 'Let us go upstairs together and see where you keep your money.' They went up to the room and counted the money and made a thorough search of the house.

When the mother saw this she could not contain herself any longer. She came out before the stranger and said: 'Baba, what has happened?' He answered in broken Hindustani that some money had been stolen.

'Stolen!' the mother cried, 'Why! How could it be stolen? Who could do such a dastardly thing?' Haralal said to her: 'Mother, don't say a word.'

The man collected the remainder of the money and told Haralal to come with him to the Manager. The mother barred the way and said: 'Sir, where are you taking my son? I have brought him up, starving and straining to do honest work. My son would never touch money belonging to others.'

The Englishman, not knowing Bengali, said, 'Achcha! Achcha!' Haralal told his mother not to be anxious; he would explain it all to the Manager and soon be back again. The mother entreated him, with a distressed voice, 'Baba, you haven't taken a morsel of food all morning.'

Haralal stepped into the carriage and drove away, and the mother sank to the ground in the anguish of her heart.

The Manager said to Haralal: 'Tell me the truth. What did happen?'

Haralal said to him, 'I haven't taken any money.'

'I fully believe it,' said the Manager, 'but surely you know who has taken it.'

Haralal looked on the ground and remained silent.

'Somebody,' said the Manager, 'must have taken it away with your connivance.'

'Nobody,' replied Haralal, 'could take it away with my knowledge without taking first my life.'

'Look here, Haralal,' said the Manager, 'I trusted you completely. I took no security. I employed you in a post of great responsibility. Every one in the office was against me for doing so. The three thousand rupees is a small matter, but the shame of all this to me is a great matter. I will do one thing. I will give you the whole day to bring back this money. If you do so, I shall say nothing about it and I will keep you on in your post.'

It was now eleven o'clock. Haralal with bent head went out of the office. The clerks began to discuss the affair with exultation.

'What can I *do*? What can I *do*?' Haralal repeated to himself, as he walked along like one dazed, the sun's heat pouring down upon him. At last his mind ceased to think at all about what could be done, but the mechanical walk went on without ceasing.

This city of Calcutta, which offered its shelter to thousands and thousands of men had become like a steel trap. He could see no way out. The whole body of people were conspiring to surround and hold him captive—this most insignificant of men, whom no one knew. Nobody had any special grudge against him, yet everybody was his enemy. The crowd passed by, brushing against him: the clerks of the offices were eating their lunch on the road side from their plates made of leaves; a tired wayfarer on the maidan, under the shade of a tree, was lying with one hand beneath his head and one leg upraised over the other; the up-country women, crowded into hackney carriages, were wending their way to the temple; a chuprassie came up with a letter and asked him the address on the envelope—so the afternoon went by.

Then came the time when the offices were all about to close. Carriages started off in all directions, carrying people back to their homes. The clerks, packed tightly on the seats of the trams, looked at the theatre advertisements as they returned to their lodgings. From to-day, Haralal had neither his work in the office, nor release from work in the evening. He had no need to hurry to catch the tram to take him to his home. All the busy occupations of the city—the buildings, the horses and carriages, the incessant traffic—seemed, now at one time, to swell into dreadful reality, and at another time, to subside into the shadowy unreal.

Haralal had taken neither food, nor rest, nor shelter all that day.

The street lamps were lighted from one road to another and it seemed to him that a watchful darkness, like some demon, was keeping its eyes wide open to guard every movement of its victim. Haralal did not even have the energy to enquire how late it was. The veins on his forehead throbbed, and he felt as if his head would burst. Through the paroxysms of pain, which alternated with the apathy of dejection, only one thought came again and again to his mind; among the innumerable multitudes in that vast city, only one name found its way through his dry throat, 'Mother!'

He said to himself, 'At the deep of night, when no one is awake to capture me—me, who am the least of all men—I will silently creep to my mother's arms and fall asleep, and may I never wake again!'

Haralal's one trouble was lest some police officer should molest him in the presence of his mother, and this kept him back from going home. When it became impossible for him at last to bear the weight of his own body, he hailed a carriage. The driver asked him where he wanted to go. He said: 'Nowhere, I want to drive across the maidan to get the fresh air.' The man at first did not believe him and was about to drive on, when Haralal put a rupee into his hand as an advance payment. Thereupon the driver crossed, and then re-crossed, the maidan from one side to the other, traversing the different roads.

Haralal laid his throbbing head on the side of the open window of the carriage and closed his eyes. Slowly all the pain abated. His body became cool. A deep and intense peace filled his heart and a supreme deliverance seemed to embrace him on every side. It was *not* true—the day's despair which threatened him with its grip of utter helplessness. It was *not* true, it was false. He knew now that it was only an empty fear of the mind. Deliverance was in the infinite sky and there was no end to peace. No king or emperor in the world had the power to keep captive this nonentity, this Haralal. In the sky, surrounding his emancipated heart on every side, he felt the presence of his mother, that one poor woman. She seemed to grow and grow till she filled the infinity of darkness. All the roads and buildings and shops of Calcutta gradually became enveloped by her. In her presence vanished all the aching pains and thoughts and consciousness of Haralal. It burst—that bubble filled with the hot vapour of pain. And now there was neither darkness nor light, but only one tense fulness.

The Cathedral clock struck one. The driver called out impatiently: 'Babu, my horse can't go on any longer. Where do you want to go?'

There came no answer.

The driver came down and shook Haralal and asked him again where he wanted to go.

There came no answer.

And the answer was never received from Haralal, where he wanted to go.